Through The Darkness

Prologue

Shadows were always in [ ] the corners of my mind, ready to take me in. S[ ] arkness surrounded me. It felt like it might swallow [ ] nd snuff out my inner light. My childhood was a patchw[ ] memories, a tapestry woven with threads of fear, pain, and betrayal.

The man who was supposed to protect me, to guide me, had instead become the very source of my torment. My father held a lot of power. He twisted that power into a weapon. He used it to hurt me and my family in terrible ways.

The abuse was constant. It was a cycle of violence and manipulation. The scars it left were too deep to heal completely. I lived in constant terror, my every waking moment filled with the dread of his return, the fear of his anger. The walls of our home, once a sanctuary, became a prison, trapping us in a world of darkness and despair.

As I grew older, the shadows grew stronger, threatening to consume me entirely. I tried to escape, to build a life of my own, but the past refused to let me go. It followed me, a spectre that haunted my every step, a constant reminder of the trauma I had endured.

Just when I thought I could break free and build a new life for my children and me, the darkness hit again. The fragile peace I had fought so hard to create was shattered, and once more, I found myself trapped.

But this time, I was determined to fight back. I would not let the shadows consume me, not again. This time, I would face the darkness head-on, and I would emerge victorious, no matter the cost. The battle ahead would be fierce, the challenges immense, but I knew that I was not alone. With my family's love and support, I would find strength to face my past and take back the life that was stolen from me.

Chapter One: Flashbacks

I find it difficult to articulate the complexities of my childhood and family. While I know there are supposedly many happy memories, I struggle to recall any of them in detail. The moments I remember feel like blurry snapshots from old cameras. They give me an unsettling feeling that the joy in them was never really mine. My grandmother would gently sit me down and flip through each photo. She shared the stories behind them and would say, "You must remember these moments, Bea." They are special. You were such a lucky girl." If only she knew the truth. She unknowingly raised a monster, treating him like a treasure. The truth stayed hidden until I wanted revenge. Deep down, I feel very inadequate. I'm not strong enough to face the monster in my memories.

I'm sitting with my grandmother now. She's going through a worn, sun-bleached cardboard box that used to hold Christmas gifts. When I was young, I kept photos in old bin bags in the loft. Later, I moved them to photo albums, but they have fallen apart, probably thanks to my kids' curious hands. Now, this box, a testament to my grandmother's online shopping addiction, sits before us. She always claims to detest online shopping, lamenting that "it's just not the same!"

"Oh look, Bea! Here's a picture of you at about seven years old. Yes, that dress—I got it for you from the YMCA. And Lucy—she must have been five! Look at her beautiful blonde hair!" I stifle a sigh. My grandmother's passive-aggressive remarks about my appearance have become a familiar refrain. In her eyes, the only people who dyed their hair black were goths or "emos," a concept she finds distasteful. She keeps admiring the photograph, her eyes shining with tears. She remembers the past, and her sun-damaged cheeks crinkle into a smile. "And Rosie—she must have been six, such a pretty girl!"

At that moment, my sister Lucy enters, a bitter expression on her face. "A blow-up doll?" she interjects, adding her usual dose of cynicism. "Lucy, must you always be so vulgar?" my grandmother chastises, her voice a mix of irritation and affection. "Bea, look at this picture—don't you remember this day? You all went to visit your dad!"

Lucy and I exchange sceptical glances, our eyebrows raised in unison. "Of course we do," we reply, though the truth is far from that. None of these photos evoke any warmth in my heart; instead, they summon a sense of dread. The dress my grandmother points out is a strange mildew green and has bronze leaves. It is definitely not beautiful. It clung to me uncomfortably, the sleeves too long for my chubby arms, and the hem barely grazing my knees. I remember my hair. It was once a stunning snowy blonde. Now, it's turning into an unappealing mousy colour. My grandmother cut it into a perfect fringe with her steady hand. In the photograph, I wore a smile that belied the horror of the day it depicted, my innocence shining through.

That night, my innocence fell apart as I confronted the monster in the shadows.

Family gatherings were often chaotic. They included distant relatives and friends. Laughter blended with the strong smell of cigarette smoke. A cheap karaoke machine, a Christmas gift from me, would be the centrepiece of our gatherings. I could never take my turn. The adults always grabbed the microphone and sang vulgar songs. I would sit quietly, humming along, my heart heavy with unexpressed yearning.

As night fell, my father would send everyone home. This left just the four of us—him, my mother, my sister, and me—in our small, cramped house. The moment the door closed, the atmosphere shifted. My mother, tired from the evening's fun, would doze off in her wheelchair, unaware of the storm coming.

"I'll get her to bed, Dad," I would offer, but he would dismiss me with a wave of his hand. My heart raced as I neared the hoist for my mother. Then, I felt a sudden, sharp pain—his hand hit the back of my head. "I counted six dirty looks you gave me. How dare you wear that slutty dress?" he roared, his presence looming like a dark cloud over me.

Tears streamed down my face as I struggled to comprehend his accusations. "Fatty, I'm talking to you! Look at me before I hit you harder!" His rage enveloped me, and I was paralysed by fear, unwilling to move. The pain in my skull throbbed, but I dared not let out a sound.

My mother, despite her inability to speak, would cry out as the blows continued. I was too terrified to defend her, too terrified to defend myself. My sister had already fled to her room, seeking comfort beneath the covers with our cat, Ketchup.

The cycle of violence went on. My father's anger spilled into the night. I watched the horror unfold, trying to protect my mother from his rage.

Chapter Two: Trust

"Bea, are you alright?" My grandmother's voice jolts me from my memories. "Just exhausted, sorry. The kids have driven me crazy this week," I lie, masking the turmoil within.

"Shall we look at these another time? I've got some crackers with your dad; he was such a funny boy..."

Inwardly, I scoff at the thought of my father, a man whose humour was overshadowed by his cruelty. "Yeah, can we just have some tea and biscuits?" I suggest, eager to escape the weight of the past.

As Lucy puts the box of photos back in the cupboard, I picture a day when I can look through them alone. I watch each image of my father burst into flames. But today is not that day.

"Bea, you're sweating. Are you sure you're okay?" Lucy's concern feels insincere, a reminder of our complicated history. "I'm fine," I reply, another falsehood rolling off my tongue. The façade of normalcy has become my daily routine, a mask I wear to shield myself from the truth.

I despise coming here, especially when Lucy is around. The fear of my father's unexpected presence looms over me, a spectre that never quite fades. I grab a few biscuits from the tin. Their stale taste brings back memories of family gatherings. Each bite reminds me of the life I want to leave behind.

Each day brings a new wave of triggers, memories crashing over me like waves. I can't enjoy a show or listen to music without the fear of being reminded of the past. The smell of some perfumes makes me panic. I feel breathless and shaky.

Liam, my partner, has seen my struggles up close. He knows about my PTSD attacks and the panic that hits me when I feel vulnerable. The first time it happened, I was lost in a childlike state, begging him to protect my mother. I didn't mean to traumatise him, and I feel a heavy guilt for the pain I caused.

The transition from my chaotic life with my ex, Peter, to the stability Liam offered was a blessing. With him, I felt safe, cherished, and free to explore intimacy without the shadows of my past haunting me.

As I finish my tea, I prepare to return to Liam and the kids, the laughter of my grandmother and sister fading behind me. I feel sad thinking about leaving, but I know I have to. I need to go before the memories of the green dress overwhelm me again.

Chapter Three Past Relationships

Liam and I have been together for a few years. Still, my past haunts me. It triggers PTSD and panic attacks often, leaving me breathless. One moment I'm riding high, and the next, I'm spiralling into an abyss, all because of a touch that turns my stomach. It's maddening. For the first time in twenty-seven years, I've found someone I can trust. Their touch doesn't make me flinch. I can undress in front of him without feeling forced, exposed, or grotesque. The trauma is unyielding. It tears at our relationship. I cannot escape the flashbacks or nightmares that haunt me every day. My father walks free, while I feel trapped in a prison of my own making.

I know what you're thinking: report him, ruin his life. But unconditional love keeps me shackled. I refuse to unleash that truth on my family; it would obliterate them. So, I carry this burden alone.

Liam and I met at work, both of us nursing wounds from our respective pasts. We were at our lowest, lacking the trust and will to face another day. He was my superior, overseeing my chaotic antics at the local rundown toy shop. I remember the moment I first laid eyes on him, clipboard in hand, accepting deliveries. I felt a spark, an undeniable pull that made me realise I wanted him. My type? It's not your typical tall, dark, and handsome. I want a strong protector—someone in charge who also has a fun side.

At the time, I was stuck with Peter, my middle child's dad, a man who embodied nothing more than geekiness. He lacked any hint of dominance, leaving me in control, which grew stale fast. I adored geek culture, like Star Wars tattoos and Lord of the Rings quotes. However, Peter's monotone ramblings really bored me.

Each day, I'd see his receding hairline, with greasy strands hanging on. His patchy, straw-coloured beard added to the look. His odour was a noxious blend of body funk and what I thought was weed. It only fuelled my resentment. I'd bend over backward for him, only to watch him let himself go, all because I'd allowed him to be complacent. I thought I was doing it for the kids, but really, I was just a pushover.

He cheated on me, of course—typical. I'd slaved away, juggling work and home while he lounged around, oblivious to the chaos he'd created. I felt trapped, like I was wasting my life with someone who lacked any sense of ambition or drive. Peter was everything I hated. He was lazy, messy, and unfaithful. He seemed happy to let me handle all our family's responsibilities.

In the early days of our relationship, my disdain for him only grew. I couldn't understand how someone could be so content with a life of monotony and complacency. His looks and behaviour made me think of him as weak and untrustworthy. I felt he didn't deserve my time or care.

I decided to leave him. I found comfort with another man, Liam. He offered the stability and passion I needed. But even this relationship was most likely doomed to fail, as the weight of my past and the chaos of my life caught up with us.

It was during this changing time that I began to see Peter in a new light. As I struggled to pick up the pieces, he was there, offering a steadfast shoulder to lean on. I watched him change. He let go of his old habits. He cleaned up his appearance and got a steady job. Now, he is focused on providing for his child.

The change was amazing, so I started to rethink everything I believed about him. The man I once disliked for being lazy and aimless had changed. He found the strength to face his demons and became a strong support for me and my children even though we weren't together.

In the chaos of my life, Peter stayed a strong-friend . He was a steady source of support. I didn't even realise how much I needed him. He was there for me, through thick and thin, never judging, never wavering in his commitment to our family.

The journey hasn't been easy, and there are still moments where the scars of our pasts threaten to tear us apart. Through it all, Peter has stayed strong. He shows that people can change. Growth and redemption are possible, even in the darkest times.

To this day, I still feel a pang of sorrow for how I treated Peter. He might have seemed aimless and unkempt at first, but he was always there for our kids. I really respect him for that. Liam changed me in some way. I'm not sure if it was my impulsiveness or something deeper inside me.

Whenever I went to pick up Harley from Peter, a twinge of guilt would strike me. I knew I had hurt him, even if he had betrayed me first. But I have no regrets in the man I chose instead, Liam's presence in my life had become a balm, a way to escape the weight of my past and the chaos that had consumed me.

Liam's dominance surprised me and awakened something new within me. It turned into an intoxicating addiction.

The intensity of my connection with Liam was like nothing I had ever experienced before. There was a raw, primal energy that crackled between us, a magnetic pull that seemed to defy logic or reason. With him, I found myself surrendering control, allowing him to guide me, to push me to the very limits of my desires.

Liam had a strong presence that excited me but also made me uneasy. When we were together, it felt like he could see right through my facade. He peeled back the layers to show the vulnerable, submissive woman underneath.

His touch sparked a fire in me that I thought was long gone. He gripped my hips and pulled me closer. His hot breath against my neck sent shivers down my spine. It ignited a hunger that was both scary and thrilling.

In those passionate moments, I would let go and be consumed by our deep connection. Liam had a way of making me feel cherished, valued in a way that no one else ever had. He whispered words of praise and love. His tone had a possessiveness that thrilled and unnerved me.

He stripped away my tough exterior and showed a side of me I had hidden for so long. With him, I felt free to explore the depths of my desires, to surrender to the intoxicating pull of his dominance. And in doing so, I found a sense of liberation, a freedom that I had never known before.

We loved our deep bond, but a shadow loomed over us—the painful loss of our daughter, Scarlett. The pain of her passing was a wound that would never fully heal, a gaping hole in our hearts that nothing could fill. In our grief, we held on to each other. Our love and devotion kept us afloat in the stormy sea of sorrow.

Liam became my rock and my salvation. He was a steady source of strength and comfort in my darkest times. And in turn, I fought to be his, to help him confront the demons that had haunted him for so long. We built a bond that went beyond a typical relationship. It became something deeper and more profound.

It was a journey filled with both joy and heartbreak, triumph and tragedy. Through it all, our connection stayed strong. It shows how love can heal, transform, and endure, even during the worst pain.

Chapter Four: The Trauma Continues

The loss of our dear Scarlett has created a deep emptiness. This sadness fills our home. Each corner reminds us of our loss—her laughter, her cries, and the gentle cooing that used to fill our days.

It's a nagging pain at the edges of our lives. It constantly reminds us of dreams that may never happen.

She left her siblings behind. They still look for her in their games, wondering why their little sister isn't there to play with them. Their questions pierce like daggers. They seem innocent, but they only deepen our sorrow. They were so excited to welcome her into our family, to play with her, to be her protectors. Now, they carry the weight of her absence, a burden that no child should have to bear. Their laughter is punctuated by moments of silence, as if they too feel the gaping void she left behind.

Every day is a struggle to find meaning in the upheaval of our grief. We navigate a world that feels colder, emptier without her. Her sweet smile and gentle presence stay with us. They mix with the painful truth that she is gone. The love we have for her remains, as fierce as ever, but it's intertwined with a sorrow that is almost unbearable. We are forever changed. We are bonded by our love and by the shared pain of losing our precious Scarlett.

As I finish my tea, I glance at my grandmother and sister. They joke about when Lucy tried ice skating and fell into some French students. I can't help but feel a chill down my spine. Lucy is still clumsy and manipulative. She hasn't changed much, even as a single mother to her son, Frankie.

Watching Frankie, a wild child, spend too much time on his gaming console is worrying. His eyes look vacant and lifeless. I offered to take him under my wing occasionally. I hoped to socialise him with my kids and show him that life is about more than fast food and video games. But Lucy hardly ever lets it happen. This is likely because of the hour-long train ride between our homes. It's baffling that no one in our family has learnt to drive.

Frankie's golden hair and bright blue eyes stand out against Lucy's dark-dyed hair. She seems to struggle with her identity. It's like she always changes to fit in, just like a chameleon. I'm left wondering who she truly is anymore.

As I tell them I need to leave, My grandmother's voice trembles with emotion. It shows how much she values our time together. I realise I need to make the effort to visit again soon. Liam is learning to drive for the kids, as navigating public transport is just too much of a hassle. I nod and say "maybe" back to their come visit again soon spill they'd always do. But I know I'll face another trip filled with bad smells and strange passengers, its too expensive to drive and I feel guilty when I don't visit regularly..

As I wave goodbye and make my way to the station, a sense of urgency pushes me forward. I just want to return home, where I can escape the haunting memories that swirl relentlessly in my mind. Sometimes, I really hate being me. My grandmother's lovely home stands out against the rough, dangerous streets. They are filled with society's lowest. This contrast reminds me of the dark past that still hangs over me.

Chapter Five Evil

Each step closer to that street corner sends a wave of nausea through me. It's the exact place where my father would arrive night after night. He would leave my disabled mother at home alone with my little sister, who slept peacefully and didn't know. He would call me with a command, his voice chilling in the dark. I crawled into the backseat of our big Citroën, a dirty duvet covering me like a shroud. The space was huge and often cluttered with my mother's electric wheelchair. I didn't feel comforted. I felt trapped and suffocated by the rancid duvet without a cover. The smell was awful. It was a disgusting mix of urine and sweat—my sweat and my urine since I had to wet myself to avoid a harsh beating for not holding it in. I was just 7, and my Peter Rabbit pyjamas—once bright white—were now a dirty grey, stained and worn from neglect.

"Are you working?" I would hear him ask as the car rolled to a stop. At three in the morning, the streets buzzed with a dark crowd. Prostitutes, addicts, and drunks filled the scene. Even the local vagrants lay in their doorways, unaware of the horrors around them. "Oh hey, Trevor, what are you after tonight? The usual?" Jodie, his regular prostitute, replied in her husky voice. It sounded as casual as if she were just serving him a drink at a pub.

She knew I was in the car; I had been in the car every-time. I had also arrived at her house many times before. On those occasions when my father did take me there, chaos always seemed to follow. He would leave me alone with Nathan, her drug-addled son. He was older than me, scrawny and dirty like his mother. He smelled of cigarettes and alcohol. His forearms were marred with self-harm scars, evidence of a tortured existence. I stared at him, his hair a patchwork of uneven lengths, clearly hacked at in a fit of desperation. As I watched him play *GTA*, I felt a chill creep down my spine. At just 7 years old, I knew I didn't belong there. I saw the chaos on the screen. Nathan ran over virtual pedestrians. Destruction followed him everywhere. Car horns blared and half-dressed women moaned around me. Their sounds created a haunting soundtrack to the nightmare I was stuck in.

Nathan was much older—about thirteen or fourteen. He would light one cigarette after another, not caring that I was there. He would taunt me, calling me names like "fatty" or "slut," words that echoed my father's cruelty. I hardly said a word to him. I was too scared to talk. My eyes were fixed on the disturbing scenes playing out on the TV. I sat quietly, watching the violence, until my father came back as if nothing had happened.

One night, everything changed. I sat there, watching Nathan laugh wildly as he shot at women on the screen. Suddenly, a loud knock at the door snapped me out of my daze. Nathan looked unfazed as he kept playing. His laughter filled the grimy room. The air smelled strongly of smoke and drugs. Three men relaxed nearby, injecting heroin into their veins. They seemed unaware of the world outside. The pounding on the door grew louder, and panic surged through me.

The door flew open, and my father rushed down the stairs. Jodie followed him, wearing only her flared jeans and no bra. He sprinted for the exit, but a heavily armed police officer blocked his path. I remember the terror that gripped me; despite everything he had done, I just wanted him to take me home. "Sir, you're not to leave the building. This is a drug raid. May I ask what your business is here?" The officer's voice cut through the air like a knife.

I couldn't take in any part of the conversation; my own sobs drowned out everything else. I didn't want him to be arrested; I needed him to take me back to my mother. She wouldn't survive without me. I trembled as I looked at the chaos around me. People were being thrown to the ground, handcuffed and helpless. Thankfully, my father spun some ridiculous tale, and somehow we were allowed to leave. I never asked what he said; he had a knack for talking his way out of trouble, whether it was debts or serious crimes.

But he never took us back home straight away and he never stopped doing this. He kept picking up Jodie on those street corners. Just like in the game, I felt the car rock and heard their guttural sounds of ecstasy. Tears streamed down my face each time, a mix of confusion and despair. I thought it was normal, but deep down, I knew it was anything but right.

After their time together, Jodie would pull back the duvet. She'd smile and tell me how beautiful I looked while I slept. But I never slept—not even when we returned home. My father would turn on Babe Station. It was one of those awful channels with women in heavy makeup showing off their bodies. He'd sit at the other end of the sofa, enjoying himself while I lay there, scared. He would hold one of my thighs. Meanwhile, his other hand searched for pleasure. It was a terrifying reminder that I had no safe place. I had no bed; my sister had one, my mother had one, and my father had his, but I was condemned to the small three-seater sofa.

Most nights, I lay wide awake, too frightened to sleep, while my mind raced with the terror of what I had witnessed. I spent the majority of my time dozing off in school, a mere ghost of a child. My attendance was poor. My father blamed it on my disabled mother. He used it as an excuse for everything.

As I walk past that grim street, darkness follows me like a shadow. It's a constant reminder of the horrors from my past. Every step feels like a dive into a nightmare. I just hope to escape the memories that try to take over.

I don't want a panic attack out and about; last time I had one in public, I was raced down to A&E with the fear I was having a heart attack. My phone is on ten percent, and I still have an hour before I'm home. Breathe in and out, isn't that what they always say? I do it every time I come down this road; there's no other route unless you want to add another half hour to your journey. It's just gone six, and I see the scantily dressed ladies, high on drugs, taking their spots at the corners. They seem braver than I am. It's dark and the temperature not even five degrees. I feel cold. I have on my fur-collared leather jacket. I'm also wearing a big grey Nike hoodie underneath. Liam's outgrown it now; he's muscular, not fat, of course.

Jodie died of a heroin overdose when I was a teenager, so I had no chance of bumping into her. I read it in a newspaper whilst working with my dad at the fish and chip bar. Now, as an adult, I feel sorry for her and her friends. But as a child, I wished pain on them. I couldn't stand watching them hurt each other and me. I can still feel the first time another man, other than my father touched me.

My father wrote an ad for him and my mother in a free classified paper. These papers often have sad, lonely men and women searching for love. I say he'd written for him and my mother, but nope, it was all about my mother. I was seven years old and was asked to proofread what he had written. My time at school was short. He feared he would get caught for the abuse he put me through. Still, I was very clever, and I knew it. I left with many an A in secondary school, surprising, I'm sure, but I loved learning; I took in as much as I could. The ad

had read:

"Horny twenty-something female looking to

add an extra person to her marriage, solely for fun

in the bedroom. Looking to try anything with a

male or female, not completely fussed. I am disabled, but my mouth and lady parts are still work-

in order. Call me as soon as possible to avoid dis-

appointment"

I remember skim reading it and just nodding to my father that it was correct. I couldn't tell him otherwise. I also couldn't say he was vile for exploiting my mother. There's no way she would have agreed; she couldn't even speak. Cerebral palsy had stripped her of everything from birth. She was able to walk up until she birthed my sister, and that's where it went downhill for her and us all as a family. She was only twenty. She's not with us anymore; she passed away ten years ago when I was 17. I don't want to sound heartless, but I was relieved. Her life had been riddled with pain. She was raped, pimped out, abused, beaten, and used for fraud. My father took away her rights when he gained power of attorney. She had to watch each day as my dad beat me and sometimes my sister. She lay there, unable to stop him from abusing me. Her emotional and physical pain from her illness felt minor next to her daily struggles. Like my sister and me, she couldn't escape it. The night she passed away, I didn't cry.

I held my sister in my arms, and as she blinked through tears, I told her it was the best thing to happen to all of us. She called me a heartless bitch. But it was true, for the most part, for me anyway. I no longer faced daily trauma to keep my mother safe. He often threatened me with care home placement or worse if I spoke out.

The same regular man and woman would visit my mother and father after that ad was published. Keith and Marie. They would arrive together once a week. At first my father made me and Lucy stay in the car for hours on end whilst they did their business. We had to hide there until we saw them leave.

Lucy and I would spend time combing each other's hair. We loved trying silly hairstyles, especially the pineapple style. We both struggled with plaits. We really tried, but it usually ended in knots. Then, we'd rip them out, pulling out a clump of hair too.

That is the only time we would really bond. We spoke about what we wanted to be as grown-ups. I wanted to be a police officer but later chose to be a lawyer. My sister dreamed of being a hairdresser, which made me laugh as she tried to plait my hair. Both miles away from what we actually do now but still what we aspire to be.

One night that Keith and Marie came around, Father asked me to stay inside, and Lucy was to stay in the car, alone. He told me to wait in Lucy's bedroom and strip down to nothing but my bare olive skin. The dress I had taken off was gifted by my grandmother just the day before.. I hadn't taken it off yet; it was an elegant party dress, the lilac silk smothered in sequins, top to bottom. I felt beautiful for once in my life, and as I took it off, the beauty faded away into a crumpled mess on the floor.

'Lay on the bed, beautiful baby; I've got a surprise for you,' my father had exclaimed.

I wasn't excited. His surprises never were good. 'And Buzzy Bea, if you don't give the man what he wants, I'll burn that ugly dress to ashes. I'll also tell your nanny you did it; she'll hate you for that. So, be a good girl and listen and obey'.

I didn't know the horror that was about to happen as I perched my chubby naked body on the bed. I had hit puberty very early, so I had breasts and the occasional armpit and pubic hair. I had to shave my legs and wear deodorant; at eight, it seemed unimaginable. This didn't help with my father's and his friends' perverted behaviours. Keith was middle-aged. Closer to sixty, I'd hazard a guess. He had black hair in a style that could give Elvis a run for his money, although it contained many a silver strand. I remember his eyes. They were wide, with black pupils set in an emerald green iris. They looked unique and frightening. They were captivating, but you could sense the evil they held. He was tall—really tall and slim. I could see his bones pushing against his skin, trying to break free, just like I wanted to, as he took off his smart, striped shirt.

'Hi Bea, wow, aren't you beautiful? I'm going to come lie down with you, okay?' His voice still rings through me like Sunday morning church bells. Deep yet soft and sweet. He was far from either of those descriptions, that's for sure. His hands were rough; he must have worked a trade on the builders yard; most men Father knew did, or security for the local nightclubs.

Father wasn't supposed to work; he got a lot of money caring for Mother, the car was free, the rent was paid by the government, and Mother raked in a lot of money from her disability. She was his very own cash machine; he was obsessed with money, and that's what motivated a lot of his days. He would leave me to look after my mother day in and day out, school days or not, whilst he worked on sites for cash in hand, all rules broken with no license, no cards, just the queen's head passed between grubby hands with no paperwork. I suppose it's why he turned me into his child prodigy, why he pimped me out to men like Keith. That night his filthy hands touched every part of my body. I winced as he pulled my hair tight between his fingers and threw my head back and placed his cold, sore-ridden, dry lips upon mine. Oh I already knew how to kiss back thanks to father, I had to oblige or worse things would happen, I dared not defend myself or play stupid. I knew it was wrong deep inside, but it was also my daily norm; of course, now I feel vile, violated, and vulgar. His brutal tongue traced down from my budding breasts down below. It felt bumpy and wrong; I remember feeling irritated like I wanted to hit him away, and I couldn't hold back the tears. This made him become aggressive; he wanted me to be enjoying myself and screamed at me to appreciate the pleasure he was giving me. He rammed his fingers into me and forcibly pushed them in and pulled them out. I cried even more as agonising physical and emotional pain raced around my body. He was stronger than Father; he wasn't gentle at all. He proceeded to rape me, and unlike Father, he didn't stop until he had finished inside me.

I had already started my periods, and I knew from what I had learnt at the time in biology that he shouldn't have, that it was very dangerous, and I could possibly get pregnant. He thanked me with a kiss on the forehead, put his clothes he'd thrown on the floor next to my dress back on, and left the room. I heard him thank my dad and tell him he'd be back again. This conversation continued, but through my sobs I didn't catch any more except laughter. This happened so many more times thereafter, by Keith and sometimes Keith and my father. Although, if Father hadn't joined in at the time, he would have let Keith finish and started on me himself. Marie only came in once, but she didn't touch me; she just watched and pleasured herself. After some time, Keith and Marie ceased their visits. Though many others came and went from the house, none had laid a finger on me again—except for my father, constantly.

You might have expected him to back off after the time he suspected I was pregnant. My periods had vanished for months, and anxiety gnawed at me. Dad forbade me from seeing a doctor, leaving me with no choice but to turn to him for answers. Asking my mother was out of the question; her silence was a cruel reminder of her helplessness. The moment I approached him, fury erupted. He branded me a slut, spitting venomous words that made it clear he believed it was all my doing. He treated me as if I were the architect of my own suffering, mercilessly punching my stomach until it was a canvas of bruises and agony. He demanded that I inflict pain upon myself daily, watching with cold satisfaction as I complied. For over a week, I lay on the floor, his heavy boots stomping down on me, each impact driving the breath from my lungs. He would drop five-litre water bottles onto me twice a day, their weight intensifying my torment. My body was a patchwork of purple bruises, and I suspected my ribs were shattered, but I dared not cry out. Eventually, my period returned, a pleasant yet cruel reminder of the cycle I was trapped in.

Chapter Six Father

I snap myself out of the memories; I can't have a panic attack in public again; I just can't. My phone battery is now 9%, and I still need to get to the blasted, piss-smelling train station. I'm so glad I don't live in this putrid town anymore. Although my childhood was painted in shades of grey, marked by the haunting shadows of my father's rage, and then losing Scarlett darkened the grey, I'm trying to paint a rainbow of light. Each day, I wear a mask of resilience, determined to shield myself. The scars on my body are hidden beneath long sleeves, while the scars etched on my heart were buried deep within. I found solace in books, escaping into stories where heroes triumphed and love prevailed. They became my sanctuary—a world far removed from the pain that suffocated me, fuck I forgot my book at home, so the train journey will be fun.

I suppose I have grown a little stronger. I have always yearned for freedom, for a life unfettered by the memories that clung to me like shadows. I moved out when I became pregnant with my eldest son, just after Mum died. I claimed to be homeless and found refuge in a bustling city, where the noise of life drowned out the echoes of my childhood. I worked tirelessly, juggling multiple jobs while nurturing my pregnant body; crazy as it seems, I always prayed for motherhood. The thought of having a child filled me with both excitement and trepidation. Would I be able to break the cycle? Would I become the mother I always longed for but never had, no fault of her own, of course? A few months later, in a mould-filled, cramped flat above a shop that stunk of old smoke and was thick with the scent of forgotten dreams, I surprisingly found refuge. I then welcomed my son, Jax, into the world. As I cradled the tiny, fragile being in my arms, a wave of love washed over me, dissolving the remnants of fear. In Jax's eyes, I saw a reflection of hope and possibility. This child would never know the darkness that had once tainted my life.

But the journey was not without its challenges. Like now, back then memories would sometimes creep in, uninvited, threatening to overshadow my joy. In those moments, I took a deep breath and reminded myself of the promise I made, to be the mother I never had. I filled our home with laughter, warmth, and unwavering love, creating a sanctuary where Jax could thrive.

As the years unfolded, Jax blossomed into a bright toddler. He often marvelled at my strength and resilience. One evening, as we sat together under a starlit sky on the dangerous balcony we owned, he turned to me, his eyes beaming with happiness.

'I love you, mummy!'

I smiled softly, my heart swelling with pride.

"I love you, my boy. I promise to always protect you."

In that moment, surrounded by the love we had cultivated, I realised I had broken the cycle. I had transformed my pain into a legacy of hope, proving that even in the depths of despair, love could flourish and heal. With a heart full of gratitude, I embraced the journey of motherhood, knowing that every day was a new opportunity to rise from the shadows and shine brightly.

I found myself on a familiar path a year or so later, welcoming another child into the world with Jax's father, Xavier. He was a different breed of monster—less terrifying than my own father but still steeped in the typical traits of gaslighting and narcissism. Our story began when we were just 14, during what felt like my first taste of freedom. I still laugh at how I managed to persuade my father to let me out of the house..

We played Manhunt, a game that ignited a thrilling sense of adventure. Xavier hung back with me, and as the rest of our friends faded into the shadows, we found ourselves drawn to one another. In a secluded corner, we kissed like it was the most exhilarating secret in the world. Those moments were pure magic—clandestine and full of youthful excitement.

To my father, I spun tales of innocent walks with my best friend, who just so happened to live next door. He was always hesitant to let me go, but perhaps out of fear or guilt over the things he did, he relented. My friend was well aware of my father's dark side, having witnessed his cruelty, particularly towards our dog. It was as if she held a key to my freedom, allowing me to escape the confines of my home, even if it was just for a fleeting moment.

Every opportunity I got, I was out with Xavier, my heart racing with the thrill of defiance. The fear of being caught by my father loomed over me like a dark cloud, but I was growing bolder, discovering a strength within myself that I never knew existed.

Xavier and I would escape to the beach every day, our sanctuary away from the chaos of home. We'd stumble upon quaint beach huts and hidden shacks, where we could laugh and share secrets away from prying eyes. My knowledge of intimacy was tainted by the abuse I had endured, leaving me hesitant when it came to physical touch. Yet, with Xavier, I found a different kind of connection.

In this secret world, I chose to explore our love in ways that felt safe for me. I engaged with him in ways that were thrilling and intimate, filled with a sense of adventure, even though we were far too young for such encounters. It was a whirlwind of emotions—a blend of innocence and passion, a bond that felt both exhilarating and complicated. I couldn't have him touch me intimately, though; I was too scared I'd react inappropriately and scare him away. I hadn't told him much at this time, not until we had our second boy, Dylan.

The first time Xavier and I crossed that boundary into adulthood (well, at least Xavier's first time) was at the tender age of 15, a moment that would forever echo in my memory. It all began with a playful banter from his father, who, upon discovering our relationship, handed him a pack of condoms with a cheeky grin. They were the kind that glowed in the dark and came in strange flavours, and we burst into fits of laughter at the absurdity of it all. It was a light-hearted moment that somehow made the prospect of what was to come feel less daunting.

Later that evening, as the sun dipped below the horizon and the sky began to shimmer with stars, Xavier turned to me with an intensity that sent shivers down my spine. "Will you fuck me?" he asked, his voice a mix of eagerness and vulnerability. My heart raced, a whirlwind of excitement and nerves swirling within me. I had never imagined this moment would come so soon, but the thrill of it ignited a fire I could hardly contain, but I was also scared, scared to be triggered, scared to be touched. I knew that very morning my father had asked me to suck his dick or he'd break my mom's small TV, the only bit of life my mom had. I remember shaking the thoughts vigorously from my mind; I knew I didn't want to ruin the moment.

We made our way to another beach hut, our secret hideaway, where the air was thick with anticipation. The hut was far from pristine; it housed a dirty, worn mattress that bore the marks of countless stories and a duvet that had long lost its cover. Broken windows allowed the soft moonlight to filter in, casting a silvery glow across the room.

As we stepped inside, the world outside faded away, leaving us in our own bubble of youth and desire. The thrill of breaking in, the illicit nature of our rendezvous, filled the air with an exhilarating tension. It felt like we were the only two souls in existence, lost in our own universe. The mattress creaked beneath us as we navigated this new territory, each touch igniting a spark, every kiss sending waves of warmth coursing through my body. In that moment, we were not just teenagers exploring our bodies; we were adventurers, diving into the depths of passion and discovery, fully aware of the risks but too caught up in the magic of it all to care. The air was thick with the salty scent of the ocean, mingling with the remnants of a moment that had felt so fun just moments before. Xavier and I had shared something intimate, a connection that had sparked with excitement. But as the thrill faded, an unsettling sensation twisted in my stomach.

   I remember feeling a warmth trickling down my leg and my heart plummeting as I glanced down. My breath caught in my throat when I saw blood seeping through my fingers, staining the fabric of my shorts. Panic surged through me like a tidal wave, and I could feel my chest tightening, each breath becoming more difficult than the last. My mind raced as I tried to comprehend what was happening.

Xavier's eyes widened in horror as he noticed the blood, and we both screamed—manic, primal cries that echoed off the walls of the hut. Fear took hold of us like a vice, and the reality of the situation crashed down around us. In that moment, everything we had just shared felt twisted and wrong, the thrill of intimacy replaced by a terror that was almost suffocating.

Without a word, Xavier bolted for the door, leaving me alone in the dim light, the sound of his footsteps fading into the distance. I was left in a state of shock, my heart pounding in my ears as the adrenaline coursed through my veins. I stumbled out of the hut, the world around me spinning as I tried to gather my thoughts.

The walk home felt eternal, each step heavy with dread. The beach that had once felt like a sanctuary now seemed hostile and isolating. I fought against the rising tide of fear and confusion, wondering what had just happened and why I was left alone to face it. The shadows of the trees loomed over me, whispering secrets I wasn't ready to hear.

When I finally reached home, I locked myself in my bedroom, seeking refuge from the outside. The familiar walls felt like a barrier against the world, but they couldn't protect me from the darkness that lurked within. My heart still raced, and the image of the blood stained on my leg haunted me, replaying in my mind like a broken record.

Days passed with no word from Xavier. The silence gnawed at me, amplifying my fear and spiralling me deeper into despair. I felt abandoned, trapped in a nightmare from which there was no escape. My thoughts turned dark, and the weight of my loneliness pressed heavily on my chest.

But it wasn't just the absence of Xavier that tormented me; it was the relentless presence of my father. He would barge into my room daily, his cruel words and actions chipping away at any remnants of self-worth I had left. Each encounter felt like another layer of despair added to the growing storm inside me. I felt like a ghost in my own life, unseen and unworthy, suffocating under the weight of his abuse.

The combination of betrayal, fear, and the suffocating pain of my home life became unbearable. I felt as though I was drowning, struggling for air in an ocean of despair. It was in the depth of that darkness, with tears streaming down my face, that I contemplated the unthinkable.

For the first time, I seriously considered taking my own life, believing it to be the only way to escape the torment that had become my reality. The thought whispered to me like a siren, promising peace and release from the pain that suffocated me.

In that moment, I sat on the floor of my room, the cold wood pressing against my skin, and I felt utterly lost. The darkness enveloped me, and I felt so alone. I had lost Xavier, I was trapped in a cycle of abuse, and the world felt like it was closing in. But just as I was teetering on the edge of that desperate decision, a flicker of resilience sparked within me. I remembered the laughter we had shared, the moments of joy that felt so distant now but were still part of me.

With trembling hands, I reached for my phone, praying that reaching out might break the cycle of despair that held me captive. I knew I had to fight for my life, not just for myself but for the hope of a better tomorrow. The path ahead was uncertain, but in that moment, I chose to hold onto the fragile thread of hope that remained, determined to seek help and find a way out of the darkness.

The phone I had been using was Xavier's old Nokia, a relic from a time when life felt simpler, and I could still reach out to someone who cared. My father was oblivious to its existence, a small mercy in a house filled with chaos. It didn't have internet access, but in that moment, all I needed was the ability to call or text. I desperately wanted to reach out for help, to call the police and escape the torment that enveloped us. I remember typing "999" into the phone, my finger hesitating over the call button, heart pounding with hope and fear.

But then, through the oppressive silence of our home, I heard my mother cry out. Her voice pierced through the air, filled with an anguish that was all too familiar. It echoed the pain that had become a constant in our lives. In a panic, I threw the phone down and rushed downstairs, my heart racing. My father had slipped out for one of his cash-in-hand jobs, leaving my mother alone, trapped in her own body.

As I entered the living room, I found her slumped in her chair, the small 24-inch TV flickering in front of her, a lifeline to the outside world that she could no longer truly engage with. Was she even watching? Or was she lost in a haze of pain and despair? Cerebral palsy had stolen everything from her—her ability to walk, to eat, to speak. All that remained were the heart-wrenching cries that filled the silence, each one a reminder of her suffering.

"Are you okay, Mum? What's wrong?" I asked, my voice trembling with fear and helplessness. I longed for her to respond, to see a flicker of recognition in her eyes, but all I received was the same vacant look that haunted our days. There was a hollowness in her gaze that cut me to the core, a reflection of the battles she fought silently every single day.

I felt a wave of despair wash over me, knowing that I was powerless to ease her suffering. I wanted to be the child who could comfort her, to wipe away her tears, but instead, I felt like a prisoner in my own home, shackled by the weight of our shared pain. With each cry that escaped her lips, the desperation in my heart grew, amplifying the sense of hopelessness that surrounded us. I couldn't save her, and I couldn't save myself, trapped in a cycle of despair that seemed never-ending.

Chapter Seven: My Mother

My mum is another person I hate to remember, not because I didn't love her—oh, I loved her deeply—but because of the profound sense of helplessness that surrounds my memories of her. She was a woman trapped in a body that betrayed her, her spirit slowly crushed beneath the weight of her illness and the relentless cruelty of my father. I often find myself haunted by the knowledge that I couldn't save her, that I stood by while the monster I called Dad wreaked havoc on her life, on our lives, all the while believing I was protecting her.

In those days, my mind was clouded by fear and confusion. I didn't report my father and his friends for the grotesque things they did, not just to me but to her as well. I told myself that speaking out would only lead to more chaos, more pain. If I said anything, what would happen to her? Would my father retaliate? Would he hurt her even more? Those thoughts consumed me, paralysing me with dread. It was a twisted loyalty, a child's desperate attempt to shield the one person who was supposed to protect me. But looking back now, I can't help but wonder if I made the right choice.

In hindsight, I realise that had I found the courage to speak up, to expose the horrors we lived with, perhaps things could have been different. Maybe my mother would have lived longer, freed from the shackles of her oppressive existence, surrounded instead by people who could care for her properly. Maybe she would have found a way to reclaim her life, to experience happiness outside the confines of our home. We would have been apart, yes, but perhaps apart would have meant happier. Free from the suffocating grip of my father's control, we might have found paths that led to healing, to joy.

But back then, I was too young and too naive to think that far ahead. I was caught in a web of survival instincts, where every decision felt like a life-or-death gamble. I could only focus on the present: the fear that my father would kill her, the terror that she would end up in a home where she would be just another forgotten soul among other miserable disabled people. The idea of her being placed in a facility, surrounded by strangers who might not treat her with the love and care she deserved, was unbearable. The thought of her loneliness and despair in a place that offered no semblance of home haunted me.

So, I kept the truth close to my heart, burying it deep beneath layers of guilt and sorrow. I wore a mask of compliance, pretending everything was okay, even as the walls of our home closed in tighter. In my heart, I wished I could be her saviour, the one who pulled her from the depths of despair, but I felt small and powerless. I was just a child, grappling with the enormity of our situation, too afraid to rock the already fragile boat.

Now, as I reflect on those years, the weight of my choices hangs heavily on my shoulders. I can still hear her voice, soft and broken, calling out for help that never came. I can still see her smile, dulled by pain and resignation, longing for a life that was snatched away far too soon. I hate remembering her because it reminds me of all the ways I failed her, all the moments I could have spoken up but didn't. Each memory is a reminder of my own inadequacies, a constant echo of the love that was never enough to save her. And while my heart aches for the mother I lost, it also aches for the child I was—a child who only wanted to protect her, even at the cost of my own silence.

Fuck, back to reality. My phone is down to 7% as I turn the corner to the train station, my heart pounding in my chest like a war drum. I quickly open WhatsApp, fingers trembling slightly as I type out a message to Liam. I tell him I'm on my way now but might not have service for a while. I ask about the kids, reminding him how much I love them all, as always. The familiar warmth of love floods through me, momentarily pushing back the shadows that loom ever closer.

But as I look up from my phone, my stomach drops. Standing outside the newsagent next door to the train station's doors is a figure I know all too well. My father. The sight of him sends a chill racing down my spine, and I feel a wave of nausea wash over me. He hasn't changed much—still overweight, his hair slicked back but thinning, the telltale signs of age creeping in. He's wearing a suit that screams of expensive taste, a stark contrast to the meagre existence he leads. It's almost comical, really, how he always wants to impress everyone with his appearance despite having so little money.

In that moment, the world around me blurs. The bustling crowd of people hurrying to catch their trains fades into the background, their laughter and chatter becoming muffled echoes. It's just him and me. My heart races, panic bubbling up from my stomach, threatening to spill over. I hadn't seen him in months, and now he stood there, a reminder of all the horrors I thought I had escaped.

I take a shaky breath, trying to steady myself, but the memories flood back—memories I've fought so hard to bury. I remember the nights of terror, the screams that echoed through our home, the suffocating weight of his presence. He had always been a looming shadow in my life, a constant threat that I could never fully shake off. The fear I had been holding in now churns violently within me, a tempest that I can no longer contain.

What is he doing here? Panic grips me, tightening like a vice. My mind races with possibilities—did he follow me? Is he here to confront me? The weight of dread settles heavily on my chest as I remember the last time we were together, how he had raged against me, his anger a violent storm that left me shattered and terrified.

I try to blend into the crowd, but it feels like a futile effort. My hands tremble as I grip my phone tightly, but even that small comfort feels inadequate. I debate whether to turn back, to run in the opposite direction, but the train station is my only escape. The thought of facing him again, of being trapped in that small space with him, fills me with dread.

As I inch closer, I can see the way he stands, arms crossed, a smug smirk plastered across his face. He's watching the people pass by, a predator surveying his territory, and suddenly, I feel like prey. My throat tightens, and I struggle to swallow, feeling the bile rise.

What if he approaches me? What if he tries to talk? I can't bear the thought of his voice, the way it dripped with contempt and cruelty. I can't go back to that life—those days of hiding, of cowering in fear, of feeling like a ghost in my own existence.

I force myself to look away, scanning the station for a way out—a train schedule, a sign, anything that can distract me from the impending confrontation. But all I see is him, a dark spectre haunting my reality. I grip my phone tighter, willing it to ring, to buzz, to give me an excuse to turn away, but it remains silent, the screen dimming to remind me of the dwindling battery.

I'm stuck, caught between the past and the present, my heart racing as I weigh my options. I could confront him, tell him to leave, to get out of my life for good. But the fear of his reaction paralyses me. I know him too well—his temper, his unpredictability. I can almost hear his voice in my head, taunting me, reminding me of how weak I am.

The seconds stretch into eternity as he notices me, his eyes narrowing with recognition. I can see the flicker of amusement in his gaze, as if he relishes the power he holds over me. My stomach churns, and I feel like I might collapse right there, the weight of dread pressing down on me.

Suddenly, I make a decision. I turn on my heel and start to walk quickly, desperately, toward the ticket counter, my heart pounding in my ears. I can't let him see my fear. I won't give him that satisfaction. I quicken my pace, weaving through the crowd, hoping to lose myself among the throngs of strangers.

"Bea!" His voice cuts through the noise, sharp and commanding, and I freeze for a moment, dread flooding my veins. But I can't look back. I can't afford to. I push forward, my heart racing as I feel the weight of his gaze on my back, the darkness trailing behind me like a shadow.

Chapter Eight PTSD

I reach the ticket counter, my breath coming in short gasps, and I quickly purchase my ticket. The attendant gives me a confused look, but I can't focus on that. All I can think about is getting away. As I step away from the counter, I glance over my shoulder and see him still standing there, an ominous figure against the backdrop of the bustling station.

The train arrives, and I rush onto it, my heart pounding. I find a seat by the window and sit down, trying to catch my breath. As the doors close and the train pulls away, I finally allow myself to exhale, my body trembling from the adrenaline. I am safe for now, but the fear lingers, a dark cloud that hovers overhead.

I pull out my phone, still at 7%, and send another message to Liam, letting him know I'm on the train. I tell him I love him again, hoping that the warmth of those words can push back the chill that has settled in my bones. But deep down, I know this isn't over. The monster from my past is still out there, lurking, waiting for the moment to strike again. And I can't shake the feeling that this is just the beginning of another nightmare.

The silence on the train is stifling, a heavy blanket that wraps around me, amplifying my anxiety. I glance down at my phone, its battery dwindling—7%, a cruel reminder that I can't listen to my favourite music, which always helps drown out the chaos in my mind. I had also forgotten my book, that comforting escape into another world where I am not burdened by my past. All I have left is a crumpled bag of half-eaten crisps, their salty crunch inadequate for the turmoil inside me, and the rhythmic tapping of a businesswoman's fingers on her laptop across the table.

She seems entirely absorbed in her work, her brow furrowed with concentration as she types away, oblivious to the world around her. I can't help but watch her, trying to fill the void with my imagination. What does she do for a living? Is she a high-powered executive negotiating deals that could change the course of her company? Or perhaps she's a freelance writer, crafting compelling narratives that captivate audiences around the world?

Her dark hair is pulled back into a sleek bun, and she wears a crisp white shirt paired with tailored trousers that exude professionalism. I wonder if she has children waiting for her at home or if she's just as lost in her own life as I am in mine. What's her name? I feel a strange connection to her, a fellow traveller caught in the currents of life, yet she seems so much more confident, so much more in control than I feel at this moment.

As I sit there, I begin to weave a story around her—perhaps she's just returned from a critical meeting with investors, her heart racing with adrenaline as she secures funding for a groundbreaking project. Or maybe she's grappling with the weight of a recent loss, pouring her heart into her work to escape the pain. I imagine her life filled with late nights and early mornings, a whirlwind of responsibilities that leave little room for joy.

I catch little snippets of her conversation with a colleague on the phone, her voice steady and authoritative. "Yes, I understand the urgency; I'll have the report finalised by EOD," she says, her tone efficient yet tinged with a hint of stress. I can't help but feel a pang of envy. She seems to have it all figured out, while I am stuck in a cycle of fear and uncertainty, haunted by the shadows of my past.

The train rattles along, and I realise my thoughts are spiralling deeper and deeper into a pit of self-doubt. Why can't I be more like her? Why can't I shake off the remnants of my childhood, the chains that bind me to a life filled with trauma? I take a deep breath, trying to steady myself, but the panic begins to creep back in, the silence amplifying my inner turmoil.

I decide to focus on the little things around me to distract myself— there's a child sitting two rows ahead, giggling as they play with a colourful toy. The sound of laughter bubbles up, a refreshing contrast to the sombre atmosphere of the train. I find myself smiling at their joy, a fleeting moment of light in the darkness.

Suddenly, the train comes to a halt, the sudden jolt pulling me from my thoughts. The businesswoman looks up, her expression momentarily startled before she resumes her typing. I take the opportunity to glance out the window, the landscape blurring by in a rush of greens and browns. There's something soothing about the view, a reminder that the world keeps moving, even when I feel stuck.

As the train lurches forward again, I feel a sense of urgency rising within me. I know I need to confront the fears that have been suffocating me, to break free from the chains of my past. I glance back at the businesswoman, and for a moment, I wish I could step into her shoes, embrace the confidence she exudes, and leave my troubles behind.

But I can't. I can't run from the monster that lurks in the shadows of my mind. I need to confront him, to find a way to reclaim my life. The train speeds onwards, and I resolve to take control of my narrative, to write my own story rather than let the past dictate my future.

With a newfound determination, I reach into my bag and pull out the bag of crisps, crunching them loudly as a distraction. The businesswoman raises an eyebrow but doesn't comment; she continues typing, her world untouched by my chaos. I realise then that while I may feel isolated, I am not alone in my struggles. We are all passengers on this train, each with our own stories, our own battles.

As I take a deep breath, ready to face whatever comes next, I notice the train approaching my destination. I can feel the weight of my past beginning to lift, replaced by a flicker of hope that maybe, just maybe, I can forge a new path forward. The doors will open soon, and I will step into a new chapter, armed with the knowledge that I have the power to change my story.

As the train comes to a stop in my hometown, I feel a wave of emotions wash over me. Stepping off the train, I'm acutely aware that the station is just a stone's throw away from where our beautiful Scarlett rests in her forever bed. Despite the dwindling battery on my phone and the urgency to get home, I know I have to see her. Today has been overwhelming in so many ways, and while Scarlett's death has cast a long shadow over my heart, she also brings me a sense of comfort and love that I desperately need right now.

Chapter Nine The Aftermath

Her absence is a wound that will never fully heal, but there's something about visiting her that feels like a balm for my soul. In my heart, I know that she didn't choose to leave us; she was just a baby, innocent and pure, untouched by the cruelties of this world. She never caused pain to anyone, and I can't help but feel that she would have brought so much light into our lives if things had been different.

I often hear people say that "God takes the best people," but honestly, that saying rings hollow in my ears. It feels like a cruel joke, a way to rationalise something that is utterly incomprehensible. God, if He exists, seems to have a twisted sense of justice. I can't reconcile the idea that a loving deity would snatch away such a precious life, leaving a gaping hole in the hearts of those who loved her so fiercely.

But as I walk toward her resting place, I let go of those heavy thoughts, if only for a moment. I'm reminded that even in her absence, Scarlett continues to be a source of love and strength for me. She is my heart, my little angel who brings warmth to my grief. Today, I will honour her memory, allowing the love I have for her to wash over me, even amidst the pain.

I take a deep breath, feeling the crisp air fill my lungs, and I step forward, ready to embrace the bittersweet comfort of being near her once more.

Scarlett's memorial area definitely needed an overhaul. The flowers had wilted, the decorations faded over time, and the whole space felt heavy with neglect. Yet, money was tight, especially after the whirlwind of emotions that came with the birth of the twins just a couple of months ago. I had only recently convinced myself to seek sterilisation after Scarlett's death, believing it was the only way to escape the cycle of grief and heartbreak.

But then came the day of my scan. I had been suffering from excruciating abdominal pain, convinced it was something dire—cysts, cancer, or some other nightmare lurking within me. My mind raced with dark thoughts as I lay on the examination table, the sterile room closing in around me. The sonographer began her examination, and I braced myself for the worst.

Instead, what I saw on the screen made my blood run cold. Those little kidney-shaped blobs were unmistakable—two tiny foetuses, squirming and kicking as if mocking my anguish. "It's twins!" the sonographer exclaimed, her voice filled with excitement that felt like a slap in the face. I couldn't comprehend her words; shock washed over me like a tidal wave. I burst into tears, overwhelmed by the tidal wave of emotions crashing down on me, and I fell off the bed in a daze.

Liam hadn't come with me; he was at home, blissfully unaware of the dark twist our lives were about to take. I was left to deliver the news, to shatter the fragile peace we had barely clung to since Scarlett's passing. The idea of bringing two new lives into a world that had already taken one felt like a cruel joke, a horrific reminder that life can be both beautiful and terrifying in equal measure. I could already feel the weight of the shadows lurking behind me, waiting to engulf us all over again.

The past two months have swept me into a relentless whirlwind of fear, anxiety, and heartache. Each day has felt like an uphill battle against my own mind, as obsessive thoughts and overwhelming pain gnaw at my sanity. The world outside seems to spin on, indifferent to my turmoil, while I remain frozen in a chaotic storm of emotions. Every time I check on my twin boys while they're sleeping, a suffocating panic attack grips me, far more intense than the ones I endured at the hands of my father. The mere thought of losing them sends chills through my spine, a visceral fear that feels all too real.

The sounds of ambulances wailing in the distance and the echoes of crashes reverberate in my mind, triggering memories I wish I could forget. In those moments, I find myself spiralling into a dark abyss, where I can't help but envision the worst—my precious boys lying lifeless, stolen away from me in an instant. Each check on them becomes a ritual steeped in dread, my heart racing as I lean over their cribs, desperately searching for the reassuring rise and fall of their tiny chests.

I know I need to be strong, to shield Harry and Olly from my fears, to keep the shadows of my anxiety from encroaching on their innocent lives. I want to protect them from my darkness, to let them experience the joy of childhood without the weight of my worries dragging them down. But it's a heavy burden to bear, this relentless nightmare that looms over us all. Every giggle, every coo, feels like a fragile moment suspended in time, and I can't shake the feeling that it could all come crashing down in an instant.

Liam tries to remain a pillar of strength, but I can see the worry etched on his face, a reflection of the turmoil we all endure together. We share fleeting glances that speak volumes—silent acknowledgements of the unspoken fears that haunt our nights. The weight of our collective anxiety hangs heavy in the air, an invisible thread binding us in this shared experience of dread. I catch him staring at the boys while they sleep, and I know he is wrestling with the same horrifying thoughts that plague me. The unspoken question lingers between us: What if we lose them?

Despite my best efforts to keep my fears at bay, I can feel them creeping into our everyday life, casting long shadows over our once-happy home. I can't help but notice how Harry and Olly seem to sense the tension that permeates the air. They are perceptive little souls, and it breaks my heart to think I might be pushing my anxiety onto them, tainting their innocent joy with my own darkness. I find myself holding them a little tighter, kissing their foreheads a little longer, as if each moment could somehow stave off the fear that clings to me like a second skin.

Even the sound of laughter in our home feels tinged with sadness. I want to join in, to be present in those moments of joy, but the anxiety churns relentlessly within me, a constant reminder of how fragile our happiness is. I try to engage with the other children, to show them love and affection, but I often find my mind drifting to darker places, imagining scenarios that send shivers down my spine.

Will it get better? Deep down, that glimmer of hope feels dim, almost extinguished by the weight of our reality. Each night, as I hover over my sleeping boys, I can't shake the feeling that this is just the beginning of a long, painful journey. I want to believe that there will come a day when the shadows will retreat, when I can look at my children without a knot of fear tightening in my chest. But for now, I remain trapped in this cycle of dread, praying for a miracle—a sign that we will emerge from this darkness unscathed, that our family will be whole again.

Taking a deep breath, the familiar ache of loss settles in my chest as I kneel down. The sun hangs low in the sky, casting a golden glow over the small patch of earth that holds my beautiful daughter. I begin to tidy up the area, gently removing wilted flowers and brushing away the fallen leaves that have gathered over time. With each movement, I try to channel my grief into something tangible, hoping that by caring for her resting place, I can somehow honour her memory.

As I work on cleaning her area, I speak softly to Scarlett, my voice barely above a whisper. "Hey, my sweet girl," I say, feeling the warmth of the sun on my back. "I've been thinking about you so much lately. Your twin brothers, Harry and Olly, are growing fast. They're so full of life, just like you were. I hope you're watching over them." I pause, imagining her smile, that radiant light that could brighten even the darkest days. "And your sister, she's just as fierce as you were. I can see your spirit in her, and it brings me comfort."

I lean closer to the grave, feeling the weight of the words I want to share. "Do you remember that day we went to the beach?" I begin, a bittersweet smile creeping onto my lips. "You were so excited to see the sand, to feel it between your little toes. But the moment the cold seawater touched your legs, you squealed and ran back to me, your eyes wide with shock. You hated it, didn't you? You thought the ocean was trying to grab you, pulling you into its depths. You clung to my leg, demanding I keep you safe from the waves. I remember how your laughter mixed with your cries, a melody of joy and defiance."

I reminisce about the way you would build sandcastles, determined to create the tallest tower, only to watch it wash away with each incoming wave. "You were so fierce, so full of life. You never let anything stop you, not even the sea," I continue, my voice trembling as I fight back tears. "I wish you could have seen how much your brothers love the water too. They splash and giggle just like you used to, but you're always in my heart, Scarlett. You're forever part of our family."

After sharing these cherished memories, I sit in silence for a moment, letting the tranquillity of the graveyard wash over me. But as the sun begins to dip below the horizon, I know it's time to leave. I blow a gentle kiss to the grave, my heart aching with the weight of my love for her, and whisper, "I love you, my sweet girl. I'll always carry you with me."

As I rise to head to the bus stop, a wave of panic washes over me. I pull out my phone to check the time, only to see the screen dim and go dark—my battery has died. My heart races, fear gripping me as I picture the twins at home. What if something happened while I was out? What if they need me? The thought is unbearable, a gnawing anxiety that claws at my insides.

I quicken my pace, urgency fuelling my steps as I make my way to the bus stop. Each passing moment feels like a lifetime, the world around me blurring as the dread settles in. I can't shake the images of my boys from my mind, the worry twisting into a tight knot in my stomach. I should have been there, should have been present for them, and now the fear of losing them too looms larger than ever.

As I finally reach the bus stop, I glance around, willing the bus to arrive faster. I can feel my heart pounding in my chest, echoing the worry that consumes me. I close my eyes for a brief moment, taking a deep breath to steady myself, but all I can think about is Scarlett and the precious life we lost. I can't lose anyone else. Not now. Not ever again.

Chapter Ten: Anxiety

As the bus pulls up, I push through the doors, the weight of panic pressing down on me. The air inside feels thick and stifling, and I'm drenched in sweat, my heart racing like a frantic drum in my chest. Each breath comes in shallow gasps, my mind a swirling void consumed by a singular, horrifying thought: the twins are dead. I can't shake the image of Liam calling me with devastating news, just like he did when Ember was taken from us.

The faces of my other children flash through my mind, screaming and crying, echoing my own spiralling chaos. The bus jolts forward, and I cling to the overhead strap, desperately trying to anchor myself to something solid as the world around me spins. The memories of Scarlett and the beach, the laughter, the joy—all of it fades away, replaced by a suffocating dread that tightens around my throat.

As the bus rattles down familiar streets, I can barely register the passing scenery. My legs feel like lead, heavy and unresponsive, as if they're betraying me in my time of need. I can't focus on anything but the horrifying thoughts consuming me. What had I been thinking, spending so much time at Scarlett's grave? How could I have let this happen?

When the bus finally comes to a stop, I leap from my seat, my body moving on instinct. I sprint toward home, my legs struggling to carry my weight, each step feeling like I'm wading through molasses. I feel weak and nauseous, the bile rising in my throat as tears stream down my face. The fear grips me like a vice, twisting tighter with every breath. I'm crying—badly crying—my sobs wracking my body, a desperate release of the pent-up terror I've been holding inside.

I burst through the front door, my voice trembling as I scream, "Where are they?!" Panic floods my words, raw and unfiltered. My eyes dart around the room, searching for signs of life, for any indication that my worst fears are unfounded. And there, sitting on the sofa, is Liam, seemingly oblivious, engrossed in the television.

"Where are they?!" I scream again, my voice cracking, the anguish pouring out of me. "How could you let the twins die? How could you just sit there?" The words tumble out in a torrent of accusation, a desperate attempt to find someone to blame for the unimaginable terror clawing at my insides.

In an instant, Liam's expression shifts from surprise to concern, and before I can process what's happening, he strides toward me. The slap comes out of nowhere, sharp and stinging, and it jolts me back to reality. "Get a grip!" he shouts, his voice cutting through the fog of panic that envelops me.

"Liam!" I gasp, the shock momentarily halting my frantic thoughts. But he doesn't give me a chance to spiral again. He grabs my shoulders, his eyes boring into mine with an intensity that shatters the chaos in my mind. "They're fine! They're all fine, I promise!"

With shaky hands, he leads me toward the living room, and I can hardly believe my eyes. There, sprawled across the carpet, are Harry and Olly, giggling and playing with their toys, completely unaware of the storm that had just raged within me. The sight of them is both a relief and a new wave of sorrow washes over me. My knees weaken, and I crumple to the floor, tears cascading down my cheeks.

"I'm so sorry," I sob, the words tumbling from my lips in a flood of remorse. I'm overwhelmed by the weight of my fear, the guilt of having doubted Liam, and of having let my mind spiral into darkness. Liam kneels beside me, pulling me into his arms, and I can feel his own tears soaking into my hair.

"I'm sorry too," he whispers, his voice thick with emotion. "I didn't mean for you to worry. I thought you needed some time. I didn't want to disturb you and your battery; it had gone, so there was no further point in me trying!'

"How is this our life?" I cry, the words laced with despair. "How is any of this fair?" The question hangs heavy in the air, a desperate plea for understanding amid the chaos we've endured.

Liam holds me tighter, his warmth enveloping me, but the reality remains. We've faced so much loss, so many trials that have shaken the very foundation of our family. "I don't know," he admits, his voice cracking under the weight of his own grief. "I wish I had the answers. All I know is that we have to keep fighting. For them. For us."

As we sit together on the floor, surrounded by the vibrant chaos of our children's laughter, I realise that despite the darkness that has threatened to consume us, there is still light to be found in our love. With trembling hands, I wipe my tears and pull away slightly, looking into Liam's eyes, searching for reassurance.

"We'll get through this," I whisper, more to myself than him. "We have to."

And in that moment, as I hold him close, I realise that while the shadows may linger, we still have each other—and our beautiful children—to guide us through the darkness. Together, we will face whatever comes next, hand in hand, heart to heart.

As I finally pull myself together, my breath still hitching as I look up at Liam, he gently shifts the conversation. "How was your trip to see your family?" he asks, his tone cautious, as if probing a wound that might still be raw.

The question hangs in the air, and my heart sinks. "It was... awful," I admit, the memories flooding back in an overwhelming wave. "Every moment felt like a reminder of everything I've tried to forget." I take a deep breath, feeling the weight of the past press down on me. "They kept showing old family photos, moments from my childhood that I would rather erase. I couldn't escape those memories—the laughter that twisted into something sinister."

Liam's expression darkens, his brow furrowing with concern. "Did you see him?" he asks, his voice low and tense. "Did your father—"

"Yes," I interrupt, my voice trembling. "He was there, not at my nan's but at the station." The confession hangs heavy between us, and I can see the fury igniting in Liam's eyes.

"Did he touch you? Did he talk to you?" The questions come out in a rush, fuelled by an anger that simmers just beneath the surface. I can feel the heat radiating from him, his protective instincts flaring up like a firestorm, and I know he's ready to confront the demons of my past.

"No! No, he didn't," I rush to reassure him, but the weight of my own fear hangs heavy in the air. "I swear, he didn't follow me home. I'm sure of it." But even as I say the words, a flicker of doubt creeps in—a shadow of uncertainty that lurks in the back of my mind.

"What do you mean you're sure?" Liam's voice sharpens, his anger palpable. "You don't know what he's capable of!" The tension in the room escalates, the shadows of our shared trauma swirling around us like a tempest.

I feel a chill run down my spine, the memories of my father's presence still fresh, like cold fingers tracing along my skin. "He didn't approach me, Liam," I insist, my voice rising in desperation. "He just sat there, smug and self-satisfied, watching me from a distance. I could feel his eyes on me, but I didn't engage. I wouldn't give him that satisfaction."

Liam's eyes blaze with fury, and I can see the muscles in his jaw clenching as he struggles to contain his rage. "I can't stand the thought of him near you, near our kids," he says, his voice strained. "I won't let him hurt you again. Not now. Not ever."

The intensity of his emotions sends a shiver through me, but there's also a sense of comfort in knowing he's ready to fight for me. "I know," I whisper, trying to calm the storm brewing between us. "I promise, he didn't follow me home. It was just a visit to the family—I thought it might help, but it only pulled me back into the darkness."

The room feels charged, the air thick with tension as we both grapple with the repercussions of my past. "If he comes near you again, I'll—" Liam begins, but I cut him off, my heart racing at the thought of further confrontation.

"I can handle it," I say, though uncertainty laces my words. "But I don't want to live in fear. I want to keep moving forward for the twins and our other gorgeous children, for all of us."

For a moment, silence envelops us, a palpable weight hanging in the air. Then Liam reaches for my hand, his grip firm and steady. "We'll face this together," he says, the softness in his voice cutting through the tension. "I won't let you fight this alone."

But as I look into his eyes, I can't shake the feeling that the shadows of my past are never too far behind. The thought of my father still lurking sends a chill down my spine. I glance toward the door, half-expecting him to come barging in, a spectre of my nightmares.

"Let's keep the door locked," I murmur, the unease creeping back into my chest. "Just in case."

Liam nods, his expression serious as he stands up, determination etched across his face. The world outside feels uncertain, every creak of the house echoing in my ears, a reminder that the past can resurface at any moment. But I know, with Liam by my side, we will face whatever comes next, even as the shadows threaten to encroach upon our fragile peace.

In an effort to reclaim some sense of normalcy, I pull out my phone and decide to order a takeaway. The comforting thought of warm food brings a small smile to my face, a welcome distraction from the chaos of the day. I glance over at the twins, nestled comfortably in their playpen, their tiny hands grasping at the soft toys I've placed around them.

Chapter Eleven

"Hey, you two!" I call, trying to infuse some cheer into the atmosphere. "We're going to have pizza for dinner!" Their wide, curious eyes follow my movements, and I can't help but laugh at their innocent expressions.

Once the order is placed, I take a moment to enjoy their quiet presence, watching as they coo and gurgle at each other, blissfully unaware of the shadows that loom over us. The sound of their tiny voices is a balm to my anxious heart, a reminder of the joy that still exists within our family, even amid the turmoil.

After a while, I realise it's time to get the other children settled for the night. "Alright, my little explorers," I say, gently encouraging them to settle down. I herded the older kids into the bathroom for their nightly routine, the air filling with splashes of water and playful shrieks as they brushed their teeth, the bathroom bustling with energy. I can't help but smile, even as the weight of my earlier fears lingers in the back of my mind.

Once the chaos subsides and the children are tucked into bed, I return to the living room. The pizza hasn't arrived yet, and I know I need something to help me unwind. I pull up YouTube and scroll through our usual videos, comforting distractions that bring a sense of familiarity.

The TV, however, feels like a minefield—each show a potential trigger. I've learnt to avoid the news, the shows filled with stories of tragedy and loss. It feels like everything I turn on is a reminder of death, of pain, and I can't bear to watch. Instead, I settle on a favourite animated series that the kids adore, one filled with silly characters and light-hearted adventures.

As the opening theme plays, I feel a sense of relief wash over me. The bright colours dance on the screen, pulling me away from my worries, if only for a moment. I sink into the couch, allowing myself to be enveloped by the familiar sounds.

Yet, even as I immerse myself in the show, a thought lingers in the back of my mind: life sometimes seems pointless. The weight of everything we've been through—the trauma, the loss, the constant fight against the shadows—makes it hard to see the light. But then I look over at the twins, peacefully sleeping in their playpen, their tiny chests rising and falling with each breath, and I feel a flicker of hope ignite within me.

They make it worth my while. Their innocence, the way they see the world as a canvas for adventure—it reminds me that life still holds beauty, even among the darkness. I take a deep breath, letting their tranquility seep into my bones, and I resolve to keep moving forward, to focus on the moments that matter.

As the pizza finally arrives, I rise to answer the door, feeling a renewed sense of purpose. I may not have all the answers, and the shadows may always lurk nearby, but I can create a safe haven for my children. I can build a life filled with love and laughter, even if it's punctuated by moments of sorrow.

I bring the pizza back to the living room, and as I set it on the table, I glance at the twins once more. In these small moments, I find my strength. Together, we will navigate the complexities of life, one day at a time, and I will do everything in my power to protect the light that shines so brightly in their eyes.

As the pizza box sits on the table, the comforting aroma wafting through the air, I feel a moment of peace settle over the house. The twins are asleep, their soft breaths a soothing reminder of the innocence that still exists in our chaotic world. I allow myself to relax, sinking deeper into the couch, grateful for the brief respite from our tumultuous lives. But that tranquillity is short-lived.

The sound of a creaking door shatters the stillness, and my heart drops. I turn to see Dylan, my second child, slipping out of his room. At only nine years old, he carries a weight that belies his age—an intensity of emotions that often feels too heavy for such small shoulders. He stands there, his expression a mixture of defiance and disdain, his dark hair tousled and eyes narrowed. In that moment, I see a reflection of his father, a narcissistic figure who once loomed large in our lives, now only mildly, leaving behind echoes of anger and manipulation.

Dylan has always been a complicated child. He was diagnosed with Pathological Demand Avoidance (PDA), a condition on the autism spectrum characterised by an extreme avoidance of everyday demands and an overwhelming need for control. This often manifests as anger, tantrums, and a deep-seated jealousy that I have struggled to understand. While he can be charming and engaging with others, he reserves his darker emotions for me, especially when it comes to my relationship with Liam and the twins.

"MUM!" he barks, his voice cutting through the air like a knife. "Why are you here? I thought you'd be with Liam and the twins as per usual! What's that? Pizza? Where's mine? How dare you forget mine!" The underlying jealousy is palpable, simmering just beneath the surface. He can't stand it when I'm alone with Liam and the twins, that it feels like I'm giving my attention to them instead of him. It's as if my love for my other children is a betrayal in his eyes, igniting a firestorm of resentment that often leaves me reeling.

In contrast, when Liam is around, Dylan is a different child. He retreats to his room, perfectly content to ignore the world until Liam has gone to work. It's infuriating, the way he can flip his behaviour like a switch, treating me as if I'm the enemy while his father remains untouched by his ire. "You're supposed to be with me!" he accuses, his voice rising. "You don't care about me anymore!"

Chapter Twelve

The weight of his words crushes me, a reminder of how much I've had to sacrifice to keep our family afloat. I've had to leave many good jobs, unable to maintain a career because of the unpredictable nature of his behaviour. The anxiety of leaving him alone with anyone, even for a moment aside from Liam, has made it nearly impossible to find stability. I can barely go to the bathroom when he's home, the fear of what might happen if I leave him unattended gnawing at me. Unless Liam is there, I can't risk it.

"Dylan, please," I plead, trying to keep my voice calm despite the rising tide of frustration. "I'm right here. I'm always here for you."

But he doesn't want to hear it. The anger spills over, and he lashes out, his words cutting deeper than any physical blow. "You don't care! You're just a stupid MOTHER who only wants to play house with Liam and the babies!" His face twists in a snarl, and I can see the hurt beneath the surface, the pain that drives his jealousy and anger.

I take a deep breath, forcing myself to remain composed. "That's not true, Dylan. I love you just as much. But I need you to understand that being with Liam and the twins doesn't mean I love you any less."

He glares at me, his expression a mix of fury and hurt, and I can feel the distance between us growing. It's a heartbreaking paradox to love a child so fiercely while also feeling the weight of their resentment. I know that beneath his anger is a child who feels abandoned, a child who struggles with emotions he can't fully comprehend.

"I don't care! Just leave me alone!" he shouts, turning on his heel and stomping back to his room, slamming the door behind him. The sound reverberates through the house, echoing the turmoil within me.

As the silence returns, I sink back into the couch, tears pricking at the corners of my eyes. The peace I had just begun to savour feels like a distant memory. I think of all the challenges we've faced as a family, the battles fought in silence, and it all feels so overwhelming. Dylan's struggles are a daily reminder of the scars our past has left, and I can't help but feel the weight of my own failures in handling the complexities of his emotions.

But I also know that he is still my son, a boy who deserves love and understanding, even when his anger feels insurmountable. I want to reach him, to help him navigate the storm that rages within, but it's a delicate dance. I can't push him too hard; I can't let his anger push me away.

With a heavy heart, I rise from the couch and make my way to his door, a longing to connect pulling me forward. I gently knock, my voice soft as I call out, "Dylan? Can we talk?"

There's a long pause before I hear a muffled "Go away!" But I refuse to back down. "I'm not going anywhere. I care about you too much to leave this like it is. Please, just let me in."

After what feels like an eternity, the door creaks open a fraction. I catch a glimpse of his tear-streaked face, anger still simmering but mixed with vulnerability. "What do you want?" he mutters, his voice wavering.

"I want to understand," I say gently, feeling my own emotions swell. "I want to help. You're not alone in this, Dylan. We can figure it out together."

For a moment, I see the flicker of hope in his eyes. It's a small spark, but it's enough to remind me why I keep fighting, why I refuse to give up on him, on us. We may be tangled in a web of emotions and past hurts, but I know deep down that love can bridge the gaps.

As I step into his room, I'm determined to navigate this storm together, one day at a time. The journey ahead may be fraught with challenges, but for Dylan, for all my children, I will keep striving to create a safe harbour amid the turbulence of our lives.

The turmoil of the evening seemed to settle for a moment, but just as I thought I could catch my breath, Dylan's mood shifted again. I watched him from the doorway of his room, my heart aching for the boy who felt so trapped in his own emotions. I stepped into the room, hoping to reach him, but before I could say anything, he lunged for the small Alexa device on his side table.

In a split second, he hurled it at me with a force that took my breath away. I barely had time to react as it collided with my face, a sharp pain erupting in my nose. The impact sent me staggering back, and I felt the warm trickle of blood begin to flow. I raised a hand instinctively to my face, shock and disbelief flooding my senses.

"Mum!" Dylan shouted, his voice a mix of anger and satisfaction, a smirk plastered across his face as he watched me. It was a look that cut deeper than the pain shooting through my nose. He didn't care. Not at that moment. All I saw was a child lost in his own darkness, but that darkness was now spilling over into my world.

Within seconds, I heard the thunderous footsteps of Liam racing up the stairs, concern etched on his face. "What happened?" he demanded, his voice booming, and I could see the anger flickering in his eyes as he approached. But as he reached me, I instinctively pushed him away. "No! Liam, don't!" I said, my voice urgent.

I knew how angry he could get with Dylan, how the rage could boil over in an instant. I didn't want to escalate the situation further. I didn't want Dylan's anger to turn into something more destructive, nor did I want to put Liam in a position where he felt compelled to confront him.

"I've got this," I insisted, holding my breath as I pressed my fingers against my nose, feeling the blood warm and sticky. Liam hesitated, his brows furrowing as he glanced between Dylan and me. I could see the conflict in his eyes, the desire to protect me battling with the instinct to shield our family from Dylan's wrath.

But Dylan stood in his room, arms crossed, a smirk still plastered across his face. He seemed to revel in my pain, his satisfaction cutting deeper than the blood pooling at my fingertips. "You're hurt, Mum!" he laughed, the sound sharp and mocking.

"Dylan, this isn't funny," I said, my attempt to keep my voice steady faltering as I felt the tears prickling at the corners of my eyes. I wanted to reach him, to show him that love still existed even amid the turmoil. I stepped forward, arms open, hoping to embrace him.

But he just laughed, a cruel sound that echoed in the room. "You're not my mum! You're just a stupid loser!" His words hit me like a punch to the gut, and I felt the fight drain out of me. In that moment, I gave up. I slammed the door behind me, the sound reverberating down the hallway as I walked back toward the living room, my heart heavy with defeat.

Liam was still there, concern etched across his features as he took in my bloodied face. "What happened?" he asked again, his voice softer now, but I could see the tension in his body. I just shook my head, willing the tears back. I didn't want to talk about Dylan right now. Not when I felt so raw and exposed.

"Let's just eat," I said, but avoiding the pizza sitting on the table. I couldn't bear the thought of eating, not when my stomach twisted in knots from the evening's events. I hurried to the playpen, where the twins were peacefully sleeping, and I quickly picked them up and settled them into their cribs, whispering soft lullabies to soothe my own frayed nerves.

Once they were settled, I wiped the blood from my nose with baby wipes, the sting of the alcohol and the pressure of the fabric making me wince. I knew I'd have a bruise, and the pain was a constant reminder of the chaos that had unfolded once again. But I didn't have time to dwell on it; I had to keep moving.

Returning to the living room, I found Liam pacing, his hands running through his hair in frustration. "We need to talk about Dylan," he said, his voice low and urgent.

I held up a hand, cutting him off. "Not now, Liam. Please." I could feel the exhaustion pulling at me, the weight of the day pressing down like a heavy blanket. I needed to focus on the twins, on finding some semblance of normalcy.

With a heavy heart, I rushed to finish the evening routine. I tucked the twins in tightly, ensuring they were warm and safe before moving back to the living room to clean up. I couldn't shake the fear that had settled in the pit of my stomach, a gnawing anxiety that kept me on high alert. What if something happened to them? What if Dylan's anger spiralled out of control?

Chapter Thirteen

As I finished up and moved to the bedroom, I slipped under the covers, exhaustion washing over me like a wave. I closed my eyes, hoping for a moment of peace, but the fear lingered. Liam joined me moments later, but I remained silent, pretending to be asleep as he settled beside me.

I could feel his warmth beside me, his presence a comfort, but I was too wrapped in my own turmoil to reach for him. The silence stretched between us, heavy and thick, as I fought back the tears threatening to spill. I knew he wanted to talk, to process everything that had happened, but I couldn't bear it. I couldn't face the anger, the frustration, and the fear that had become my constant companions.

Instead, I lay there, listening to the soft sounds of the night—the distant hum of the neighbourhood, the gentle breaths of my family, and the weight of my worries pressing down on me. I knew I should speak, should let him in, but the fear of what might come next kept me locked away in my own silence.

And as the minutes ticked by, I felt the darkness creeping back in, wrapping around me like a shroud as I contemplated the battles I would have to face tomorrow and the uncertainty that lay ahead.

As I lay beneath the covers, the weight of the night pressing down on me, my thoughts spiralled into darker territories. I couldn't shake the feeling that something was amiss with Dylan—something deeper than the Pathological Demand Avoidance diagnosis he carried. I found myself wondering if he had inherited more than just his father's anger. What if there was something more sinister lurking beneath the surface?

I couldn't help but draw parallels between Dylan's struggles and the patterns I had witnessed throughout my own family. My father's volatility had always been a shadow over my childhood, a constant reminder of how easily anger could erupt. And then there was his father, whose narcissism and manipulation had left scars not just on me, but on everyone around him. Was Dylan caught in the same web of inherited pain and chaos?

My thoughts drifted to my mother's mother, who battled schizophrenia. The memories of her were fragmented and terrifying, a kaleidoscope of images that filled me with dread and sympathy. I could still recall the way she would stare blankly at the walls, lost in her own world, her eyes filled with a haunting mix of fear and confusion. There were moments when I felt sorry for her, trapped in a mind that twisted reality into something grotesque, especially when my father would exploit her condition for money. I could see him, the way he'd charm her with his boyish smile, encouraging me to sit in the front of the car, fluttering my eyelashes and playing the cute granddaughter. It felt like a performance—one that always ended with her handing over cash, her fragile state making her an easy target.

I remembered one visit vividly, stepping into her house and being overwhelmed by the clutter. Photographs of Elvis Presley covered the walls. The King's image filled many frames, showing her delusions. She believed she was married to him, her stories swirling around me like a fog. I often wondered if her obsession helped her escape her painful reality. Maybe marrying a rock star was her way to find happiness in all the chaos.

One day, she sat me down, her voice shaking as she recounted a story that still haunted my nightmares. "You know," she said, her eyes wide with fear, "my husband—he was a monster. He once murdered our child by throwing him against the wall." The words hung in the air, chilling me to the bone. I remember staring at her, trying to understand the horror of her words. My heart raced as I realised she was talking about a reality that had once been hers.

I felt so small in that moment, as if the weight of her pain had settled onto my shoulders. I thought about how someone could feel such deep sadness. I also wondered how a family could fall apart so completely. Losing a child feels real now. Back then, the thought of seeing such brutality seemed impossible and unbearable. A shiver ran down my spine as I thought about the trauma in my family. It felt like a dark river flowing through our history.

Dylan's behaviour echoed with those shadows, and I couldn't help but worry. What if there was more than just PDA at play? What if he carried the weight of generational pain? What if anger and violence echoed through our bloodline? The thought chilled me. I felt I had to protect him and guide him through the darkness ahead.

As I lay there, I felt a surge of anger at the circumstances that had shaped our lives. I felt anger at my father for the chaos he caused. I was also angry at my mother for not protecting us. But she couldn't. I was upset with fate too, for putting such burdens on my children. I wanted to change the story for Dylan. I didn't want him to face the same despair I saw in my family.

But how? How could I navigate this labyrinth of emotions and fears? I felt so lost in my thoughts, the tears I had held back now spilling over as I faced the reality of what lay ahead. I wanted to reach out, to pull Dylan back from the brink, to show him that love existed, even in the shadow of darkness.

Suddenly, I felt a warm hand on my shoulder, and I turned to see Liam watching me, concern etched across his face. "You okay?" he asked softly, his voice a comforting balm against the turmoil inside me.

I shook my head. I felt sorrow as I thought about Dylan and the patterns that repeated through the years. I thought about my grandmother's struggles. She fought schizophrenia, and my father controlled her. The haunted stories still echoed in my mind.

"I can't help but wonder if Dylan is going down that path," I admitted, my voice trembling. "What if he inherits more than just anger? What if there's something darker lurking beneath the surface?"

Liam listened intently, his eyes filled with empathy as I poured out my fears. "You're not alone in this," he said gently, squeezing my hand. "We'll figure it out together. You're doing everything you can for him. You're a good mum."

But even as he spoke those words, doubt gnawed at me. I felt the weight of the past pressing down, a suffocating reminder of the legacies that had shaped us. And as I lay there, my heart heavy with worry, I knew that the road ahead would be fraught with challenges. But I also knew that I wouldn't face it alone. We would join forces to change the story. We want to fill it with love, understanding, and hope for a better future.

I tried to get back to sleep, hoping exhaustion would help. I needed a break from the storm of thoughts in my mind. But sleep eluded me, slipping through my fingers like sand. I lay there, my heart racing. Every slight sound from the corner of my room, where the twins slept, made me bolt upright in bed. My breath caught in my throat.

It was a nightly ritual—an anxiety-laden performance that I couldn't escape. I climbed out of bed at least a hundred times, the fear clawing at my insides like a wild animal. I would often look at the twins in their cribs. I checked to see if they were still breathing. Their tiny bodies rose and fell with each precious breath.

My mind often replayed the haunting memory of Scarlett, my sweet girl who had been taken from us too soon. The weight of that loss felt heavy, like a dark cloud. It reminded me how fragile life is. Every time I checked on the twins, the fear would wash over me anew—what if something happened to them? What if I couldn't protect them from the same fate that had befallen Scarlett?

After what seemed like hours of restless checking, I finally fell back into bed, my heart still racing. But the peace I craved was elusive. I felt trapped in a cycle of fear and worry, my mind racing with thoughts I couldn't quiet. I couldn't carry on like this.

Feeling desperate, I tossed the covers aside and dashed down the stairs. My feet moved like they were controlled by an invisible force. I stumbled into the bathroom, flicking on the light, and flinched at the sight of my reflection in the mirror. My nose was swollen and bruised from Dylan's outburst. Blood had dried at the edges, and my tear-stained cheeks were puffy and red. I looked like a ghost of myself, a shadow lost in the depths of despair.

As I stared at my reflection, a wave of hopelessness crashed over me. The thought hit me hard: what if everyone would be happier without me? The weight of that question pressed down on my chest, suffocating me. I felt as if I was a burden to my family, a source of chaos and fear. My mind spiralled into dark corners. Thoughts swirled like a tempest, ready to pull me under.

I thought of my children—of Dylan and his anger, of the twins and the fear I held for them. I thought about how hard I'd fought for a loving home. Yet, here I was, standing in the bathroom with my heart shattered and my spirit crushed. Would they be better off without the weight of my pain? Would they flourish in a world free of my anxieties and fears?

Tears streamed down my face as I leaned against the sink, the cold porcelain grounding me in the moment. My heart ached, a deep, hollow pain that resonated through every part of me. I felt utterly alone, lost in a sea of swirling emotions, drowning in despair.

"Why can't I be stronger?" I whispered to myself, my voice barely a sound above a breath. "Why can't I just get it together?" But the questions went unanswered, echoing back at me in the empty room.

I closed my eyes and let the tears fall. Sobs shook my body as I thought about all I had been through. The pain of losing Scarlett, the struggle to navigate Dylan's anger, and the fear of failing the twins. It all felt like too much, a mountain I couldn't climb.

The moment stretched on, and I found myself wishing for an escape. An escape from the pain, the heartache, the constant worry that had become my everyday reality. I stood on the edge, looking into a deep void that seemed to offer relief. But I knew it was the wrong choice. I couldn't abandon my children, even if the thought felt tempting.

With a shaking hand, I wiped my tears away and took a deep breath, trying to ground myself in the present. I had to keep moving forward. I had to keep fighting, not just for myself, but for my children. They needed me, even if they didn't always understand it. They needed my love, my guidance, and my strength.

As I stood there, I realised I had a choice. I could succumb to the darkness that beckoned, or I could choose to fight against it. I could lean into the love I had for my children, even when it felt like the world was crashing. down around us.

I stood tall and looked at my reflection. I whispered, "I won't give up." The words felt strange, but I knew I had to believe them. I had to keep pushing forward, one step at a time.

I stepped away from the sink, taking a moment to collect myself, and turned off the light. As I walked back upstairs, the weight of the world still pressed on me. But a flicker of hope sparked inside. I would face the challenges ahead, and I would do it for my children—because they were worth every ounce of my fight.

I climbed back into bed, the covers wrapped around me like a shield. Sleep still eluded me, but I felt a bit less alone. I knew I had to face the darkness trying to take over me. But I also had to cling to the light—the love of my children, Liam's support, and hope for a brighter tomorrow. In that moment, I decided to fight for them. I wanted them to feel the love that united us, even amid great pain.

As dawn broke, the first rays of sunlight filtered through the curtains, casting a soft glow over the room. I sat up slowly, the weight of the night still lingering in my chest. The quiet morning felt so different from the chaos of last night. I welcomed it, hoping for a fresh start. But the reality of the day ahead loomed large in my mind.

I glanced over at the twins, still peacefully sleeping in their cribs in the far corner of the room. Their soft breaths were a comfort, grounding me in the moment. I took a deep breath, reminding myself of the love that filled our home, even amid the challenges we faced.

As I prepared for the morning rush, the familiar routine began to unfold. I moved through the house, waking the older children one by one. Ariel was first, her long hair tousled and eyes still heavy with sleep. She stretched and yawned, a smile breaking across her face as she caught sight of me. "Morning, Mum!" she chirped, her sunny disposition brightening the room.

Next was Jax, who shuffled in, still half-asleep but always ready to help. "What do you need me to do?" he asked, his voice thick with grogginess. I appreciated that he was willing to help. It made our busy mornings easier.

Peter and Harley followed, bringing their own unique energy into the mix. Peter was lively and outspoken. He loved to join in playful debates. In contrast, Harley was quieter and more reserved. At just five, Harley was a little genius. His mind was full of knowledge that often amazed everyone, even his oldest brother.

As I prepared breakfast, I felt the familiar pang of concern for Dylan. He was still asleep, likely exhausted from the emotional turmoil of the previous day. But as I considered the day ahead, I couldn't shake the feeling that sending him to school felt pointless. Because of his Pathological Demand Avoidance, he struggled to meet classroom expectations. He was only allowed to attend for two hours at a time, and even that felt like a chore for him.

The system was failing him, and I felt the frustration building within me. Dylan was kicked out of several schools. He often acted violently and refused to follow rules. I knew this wasn't who he was at his core; he was a bright, intelligent boy who had so much potential. But the anger and chaos he carried made it difficult for anyone to see past the surface.

As the older children finished breakfast, I watched them interact, their differences striking. Ariel was kind and caring. She always looked out for her siblings, even though she was the youngest, apart from the twins. Jax, the oldest, was fiercely protective. He stepped in whenever he sensed someone was feeling down. Dylan was the joker. He lifted everyone's spirits with his humour but lacked empathy. Harley, who is also on the autism spectrum, had a unique talent for connecting deeply with others. X

Yet, as I observed them, I couldn't help but feel a sense of concern for Dylan. I knew all children were different. However, his struggles worried me more and more. Harley, for all his quietness and social awkwardness, had a sweetness that drew people in. He sometimes stuttered and stims when he felt overwhelmed. Still, his brilliance showed in surprising ways.

The only similarity between Dylan and Harley was their intelligence. Harley and Dylan were both very clever. Harley's brilliance was gentle and subtle. In contrast, Dylan's was often hidden by his anger and defiance. It seemed like a cruel twist of fate. The two brothers were alike in smarts but very different in temperament.

As I stood in the kitchen, preparing to send the older children off, I felt a wave of sadness wash over me. I longed for Dylan to experience the same joy and support that his siblings had at school. I wanted him to thrive and find friends who valued him for who he was, not as a problem to manage.

"Right, everyone, get your things together," I called, trying to keep the mood light. "We don't want to be late!" The children sprang into action, gathering their bags and preparing for the day. I felt a sense of pride watching them; they were all so unique, each with their own strengths and weaknesses.

As we made our way to the front door, I pulled them into a tight group hug, feeling the warmth of their bodies against mine. "Look after each other, alright? You know how important it is to stick together," I reminded them, my heart swelling with love and worry all at once.

They nodded, and with that, they were off, disappearing down the path to catch the bus. I watched them go, a bittersweet smile on my face. Despite the challenges we faced, there was so much joy to be found in their laughter and camaraderie.

Turning back to the house, I felt the familiar heaviness settle in my chest again. I knew I needed to check on Dylan. As I made my way to his room, I could already feel the tension building inside me. The worry for him weighed heavily; I was all too aware of the battles he faced.

As I entered his room, I found him still asleep, tangled in his bedsheets. I knelt beside him, gently brushing a strand of hair from his forehead. "Dylan, love, it's time to wake up," I said softly, my heart aching at the sight of him. I wanted so badly for him to find peace, to feel understood in a world that seemed so intent on pushing him away.

He stirred but didn't fully wake, his brow furrowing as he turned away from me. My heart sank; I knew this would be a struggle. I sat on the edge of his bed, contemplating how to encourage him to get up for the day. I thought about the school system. It seems stacked against kids like him. They often lack the resources and understanding to help children with PDA succeed.

After a few moments, I decided to try a different approach. "How about we make your favourite breakfast together?" I suggested, hoping that the promise of food might coax him out of his slumber.

At the mention of breakfast, his eyes fluttered open, and he groaned softly. "I don't want to go to school," he mumbled, his voice thick with sleep and reluctance.

"I know, sweetheart. But we can try to make it through today together, alright? Just a couple of hours, and then you'll be home again. "I promised him we'd have fun later," I said. I felt sad about how hard it was for him to meet everyone's expectations.

He finally sat up, rubbing his eyes, and I felt a flicker of hope. "Okay," he replied, his voice still groggy but less resistant than I anticipated.

As we headed to the kitchen, I couldn't help but feel a sense of determination surging within me. I would keep fighting for him. I'd advocate for his needs and find ways to help him navigate the world. We were in this together, and I would not give up on him.

The morning was its usual chaos, but I felt hopeful. I watched Dylan slowly get involved with the activities around him. It would be a long journey. Still, I was determined to show him he was loved. He would have support, no matter what challenges we faced. Together, we would face the day, one step at a time.

As we reached the front door, I aimed to keep things cheerful. I hoped a warm breakfast would help Dylan start the day better. Dylan suddenly paused in his step , his brow furrowing in thought.

"Mum, is Liam home?" he asked, his voice a mix of hope and expectation.

I felt a small pang in my heart. "No, love. Liam's gone to work already," I replied gently, trying to keep my tone upbeat. But as soon as the words left my lips, I could see his expression change. The light in his eyes dimmed, replaced by a darkness that seemed to seep into the room.

His demeanour changed suddenly. I watched in disbelief as he started to laugh manically. The sound sent shivers down my spine. "Liam's not here? Good! I don't need him!" he shouted, his voice rising with each word.

"Dylan, please, let's not start this," I pleaded, trying to catch his gaze. My heart sank as he turned away from me, focusing instead on his own chaos.

"Look at your stupid nose!" he cackled, pointing at the bruise that marred my face. His laughter rang out, sharp and mocking, and I felt the sting of his words deep in my chest. "Did you get that from playing with the babies? You're so weak!"

The hurtful comments cut through me, and I took a deep breath, trying to maintain my composure. I knew he was acting out, but it felt like a betrayal to see him revelling in my pain. "Dylan, I know you're upset, but we need to get ready for school. It's important," I said, hoping to redirect him.

But my words fell on deaf ears. He was already darting around the kitchen, energy surging through him like a wild storm. "I'm not going to school! You can't make me!" he shouted, his laughter echoing through the halls.

In a burst of manic energy, he ran around the house, shouting the twins' names as if trying to wake them from their peaceful slumber. "Wake up, babies! Wake up! Mum's a loser! She can't even go to school!"

I felt a surge of panic as I realised the commotion was waking the twins. "Dylan, please!" I called after him, my voice rising in desperation. "You need to stop this! You're waking the babies!"

But he was lost in his own world, the chaos consuming him as he continued to shout and laugh. I watched helplessly as the twins stirred in their cribs, their sleepy faces scrunching up with confusion. I felt a knot tightening in my stomach; I couldn't let his behaviour escalate any further.

"Dylan, enough!" I said firmly, my patience fraying at the edges. I moved to intercept him, blocking his path. "You need to calm down right now. This isn't how we handle things."

He stopped, staring at me with a mix of defiance and mischief, the laughter still bubbling beneath the surface. "And what if I don't want to?" he challenged, crossing his arms defiantly.

"Then we can't move on and you won't get to play with your phone later," I threatened, trying to appeal to his sense of logic, even though I knew it was a long shot.

But as I spoke, I could see the glimmer of mischief in his eyes. He was so caught up in his own feelings that he was beyond reason. "I don't care!" he shouted, throwing his head back and laughing again, the sound filling the room like a dark melody.

The twins, now fully awake, began to cry, their little faces scrunching up with distress. I felt my heart sink further, torn between the need to calm Dylan and the urgent desire to comfort the babies. "Dylan, you're scaring them!" I exclaimed, rushing towards the twins.

As I reached their cribs, I could feel the weight of the morning pressing down on me, the frustration and fear swirling within me. I cradled one twin in each arm, trying to soothe their cries as I glanced back at Dylan, who was still bouncing around the room, lost in his manic energy.

"Please, Dylan," I said softly, my voice trembling with emotion. "I need you to help me. I need you to be a good big brother right now."

He paused for a moment, the laughter fading slightly as he considered my words. But the darkness still lingered in his eyes, and I knew it would take more than just encouragement to pull him back from the edge.

"Do you want to help me calm the babies down?" I asked, trying to appeal to any shred of empathy that might be buried beneath the chaos.

He hesitated, glancing at the twins, who were still crying. I held my breath, praying he would respond. Slowly, he seemed to process my words, the defiance flickering just a bit.

"Fine," he muttered, crossing his arms again but this time with less conviction. "But I don't want to go to school!"

"Let's take it one step at a time," I replied, relief washing over me as I saw the smallest glimmer of understanding in his eyes. "First, let's calm the twins, and then we can talk about school, yeah?"

With that small victory, I felt a flicker of hope igniting within me again. It was a long road ahead, and I knew we would face many more struggles, but for now, we had a moment of connection.

As the chaos of the morning unfolded, I managed to coax Dylan out of his room, though not without a struggle. He emerged in his usual dishevelled state, still wearing his pyjamas and stinking of early puberty. The unmistakable scent of adolescence mixed with the remnants of a late-night snack lingered in the air around him. I winced at the sight, knowing he should have been dressed in his school uniform, but at that moment, I was just grateful he was up and moving.

"Come on, love, we need to get going," I urged, gently guiding him towards the front door. I could feel the tension in my chest tightening as I prepared for the school run. It was a task I dreaded; the teachers always seemed to be watching me, judging the way I handled Dylan's behaviour. They didn't understand the intricacies of PDA or the challenges we faced each day. It felt like every drop-off was an examination of my parenting skills, a public display of our struggles.

Once we were finally out the door, I made my way to the buggy where the twins were waiting, their little faces brightening as they saw me approach. I quickly strapped them in, feeling a sense of relief wash over me as I secured them for the journey ahead. "Alright, let's go!" I said, trying to keep my voice upbeat despite the heaviness in my heart.

We set off down the street, Dylan walking beside me, his mood fluctuating as we neared the school. I kept glancing at him, hoping for a glimmer of excitement or at least a hint of compliance. But the closer we got, the more I could see the tension building within him. I felt the familiar pang of sadness; I wished things could be different for him, for all of us.

When we reached the school gates, I took a deep breath, preparing myself for the inevitable. "You'll be alright, Dylan," I said softly, trying to instil a sense of confidence into both of us. He merely shrugged, his eyes darting around as if searching for an escape.

"Remember, just two hours," I reminded him. "And then we can have some fun afterward."

He nodded, but the defiance lingered in his stance. I walked him to the entrance, feeling the weight of the teachers' gazes on us. I could hear whispers, and I couldn't help but wonder what they were saying. Did they blame me for his behaviour? Did they think I was not doing enough? I fought back the tears threatening to spill over as I dropped him off, watching him shuffle into the building, his shoulders hunched.

With a heavy heart, I turned away and headed back towards the twins, who were babbling away happily in their buggy. I decided to take them on our daily two-hour walk, hoping the fresh air would clear my head. As we strolled through the park, I tried to focus on the beauty around us—the vibrant flowers blooming, the laughter of children playing, and the gentle rustle of leaves in the breeze. But even amidst the beauty, a shadow loomed over me.

After what felt like an eternity of walking, I found a bench and sat down to catch my breath, the twins gurgling contentedly beside me. I pulled out my phone, glancing at the time and trying to distract myself. Just as I began to feel a sense of normalcy, my phone rang, shattering the moment of peace.

It was the school. My heart sank as I answered, bracing myself for the news. "Hello, this is Mrs. Thompson from Highfield School. I'm afraid we have a situation with Dylan," she said, her tone all too familiar.

My stomach dropped as she went on to explain that he had smashed up a classroom and broken other students' property. "We'll need you to come and collect him," she added, her voice laced with a mixture of concern and professionalism.

A wave of sadness washed over me as I hung up. I felt the familiar ache in my chest, a mix of frustration and helplessness. Why couldn't he find a way to express himself without resorting to violence? Why did it always have to end like this? I thought of Dylan, sitting alone in a room, likely feeling the weight of shame and confusion. I wished I could fix everything with a magic wand, to make it all better for him, for our family.

As I pushed the buggy back towards the school, my mind raced with thoughts of how to manage this situation. I had considered sending Dylan to a home, a place where he could receive the support he needed, but the thought sent shivers down my spine. I shook it off, just as I had with my mother. I was the protector of my family; I would find a way to make this work, to give Dylan the love and guidance he needed.

But as I approached the school gates again, a heavy gloom settled over me. I hated this part of my day—the part where I had to confront the reality of Dylan's struggles and the judgement that often accompanied them. I felt the eyes of the teachers upon me as I walked through the doors, the familiar sensation of being scrutinised creeping back in.

As I entered the office, I could see Dylan sitting in a chair, his head down, his body tense. He looked so small in that moment, and my heart broke for him. I approached slowly, and he glanced up, the defiance replaced by something softer, a flicker of regret perhaps.

"Hey, love," I said softly, kneeling beside him. "What happened?"

He shrugged, avoiding my gaze. "I don't know," he mumbled, his voice barely audible.

I could feel the weight of the world pressing down on me as I placed a comforting hand on his shoulder. "I know it's tough, but we need to talk about this. We can't keep doing this, Dylan."

He nodded, and for a brief moment, I felt a glimmer of hope once again . Maybe we could work through this together. As I signed him out, the reality of our situation hung heavy in the air. I knew we were facing a long road ahead, filled with challenges and heartaches, but I was determined to walk it with him.

As I made my way back home with Dylan, the twins happily babbling beside us, I felt the weight of the world pressing down on my shoulders. How could all of this responsibility rest solely on me? I was exhausted—physically, emotionally, and mentally. The relentless cycle of worry, frustration, and heartache was beginning to take its toll.

Dylan's father, Xavier, had long since distanced himself from the chaos of our lives. He showed little interest in Dylan, preferring to focus on Jax, who, in his eyes, embodied everything he deemed "normal." Jax was kind and caring, attributes Xavier seemed to prize above all else. It was as if he couldn't bear to look at Dylan, who, in his opinion, represented everything he didn't want to acknowledge. Maybe it was because Dylan and Xavier were so similar in temperament—spirited, fiercely intelligent, yet prone to outbursts that often drove people away. Xavier likely saw in Dylan a reflection of himself, and that was a truth he was unwilling to confront.

Xavier had a way of casting shadows over our lives. When we were together, the excitement of our early love had been intoxicating, filled with passion and possibility. But that thrill faded over time, transforming into something darker, something I never anticipated. After my mother died, everything changed. Grief wrapped around me like a suffocating blanket, and the move to the flat above the shop only amplified the sense of isolation I felt. The walls seemed to close in on me, and the weight of the world became unbearable.

It was during this time that Xavier's true nature began to emerge. What had once been gentle teasing morphed into scathing remarks, and the loving gestures turned into sharp criticisms. He would often say things that cut deep, comments cloaked in the guise of humour that would leave me reeling. "Dylan is your karma," he would laugh, his eyes glinting with a mix of amusement and disdain. "You brought this on yourself."

Those words echoed in my mind, reverberating with a painful truth. In some twisted way, I think he believed it. He took pleasure in my suffering, relishing the chaos that surrounded us. When Dylan struggled, when he lashed out, it only served to fuel Xavier's contempt. I often wondered if he saw Dylan as a burden, a reminder of the life he had chosen to leave behind—one filled with responsibility and unpredictability.

As the years went by, Xavier's indifference became more pronounced. He was emotionally absent, retreating into his own world while I was left to navigate the storm alone. The love that once bound us together became a distant memory, overshadowed by a series of emotional abuses that chipped away at my spirit. I felt trapped in a cycle of despair, where the promise of a bright future was replaced by a grim reality.

I remembered the nights when I would lie awake, listening to the sounds of silence, wishing things were different. Wishing that Xavier would take an interest in our family, in Dylan. But he remained steadfast in his avoidance, preferring to spend time with

Jax, who basked in his father's approval. I could see the way Jax lit up when Xavier praised him, the way he sought his father's attention with an eagerness that broke my heart.

"Why can't you be more like Jax?" Xavier would often say to Dylan, his voice dripping with disappointment. "He's the one who makes me proud." Those words would cut through me like a knife. In that moment, I would see Dylan's spirit dim, the defiance in his eyes flickering out as he absorbed the weight of his father's judgement.

I often felt like a lone warrior, fighting for my children in a world that seemed to conspire against us. I had to be strong, to be the anchor in the storm, but the burden was becoming unbearable. The thoughts of sending Dylan away, of finding him a place where he could receive the support he needed, would surface occasionally, only to be pushed aside by the fierce love I had for him. I was the protector of my family, and I would not abandon my child, even when the thought crept in as a desperate escape.

We reached home, and I parked the buggy in the hallway, the weight of my thoughts still heavy in my mind. I glanced at Dylan, who was staring blankly at the floor, lost in his own world. I felt a pang of sadness for him, for the struggles he faced, and the way his father's absence had shaped his life.

As I settled the twins in their play area, I turned to Dylan, who still looked so small, so vulnerable. "Dylan, I want to help you," I said softly, trying to break through the wall he had built around himself. "I know things are hard, but we can work together. You're not alone in this."

He looked up at me, his eyes filled with a mixture of confusion and defiance. "Why should I care?" he muttered, the anger bubbling just beneath the surface.

"Because I care," I replied, my voice steady. "I love you, and I believe in you. We can figure this out together, I promise."

As he turned away, I felt a flicker of hope. I knew the road ahead would be long and fraught with challenges, but I was determined to fight for my family. I would not let the darkness consume us, and I would not let Xavier's indifference define our lives.

With renewed determination, I resolved to be the advocate Dylan needed, to seek the support he deserved, and to create a brighter future for all my children. I was their protector, and I would not rest until I had done everything in my power to ensure they thrived, no matter the obstacles we faced.

As I watched Dylan's defiance simmer beneath the surface, something in his expression shifted. It was as if a veil had been lifted, revealing the raw emotion that lay hidden beneath his anger. He took a deep breath, his voice trembling as he spoke. "I miss Scarlett," he said, his words barely above a whisper.

The admission hit me like a punch to the gut. I felt my heart tighten at the mention of our baby girl, the sister who had been taken from us far too soon. "I know, love," I replied gently, my voice softening as I approached him. "We all miss her."

Dylan's eyes flashed with a mix of pain and anger. "I'm scared to sleep," he continued, his voice quivering with emotion. "What if I don't wake up? What if she's gone forever?"

The weight of his words settled over me like a heavy cloak, and I could feel the tears welling up in my eyes. I had known he struggled, but to hear him voice his fears so openly was both heartbreaking and enlightening. "Dylan, it's okay to be scared. It's normal to feel that way when you've lost someone you love," I said, wishing I could wrap him in my arms and shield him from the pain.

But then, the conversation took a darker turn. "I hate Liam," he spat, the venom in his words shocking me. "He's the reason she's gone. If he hadn't been there, she'd still be here with us."

My heart sank. I had always feared that Dylan might blame Liam for Scarlett's death, but hearing it out loud was devastating. I shook my head, struggling to find the right words. "Dylan, it wasn't Liam's fault. It was an accident. You know that, don't you?"

"I don't care!" he shouted, his anger bubbling over. "And I hate the twins too! They're not her! They'll never be her!"

The pain in his voice was raw and unfiltered, and I felt as if I had been struck by lightning. I had always known that Dylan felt overshadowed by the twins, that their arrival had stirred up a whirlwind of emotions within him, but to see how deeply it affected him was overwhelming. I could see now that he felt replaced, as if the twins were a constant reminder of what he had lost.

"Dylan, listen to me," I said, my voice steady but filled with urgency. "The twins are not a replacement for Scarlett. They're your siblings, and they love you. We all love you. Losing her doesn't mean we love you any less."

But he turned away from me, the anger still etched on his face. It was clear that the wounds ran deeper than I had realised, and I felt a wave of sadness wash over me. I needed to help him process these feelings before they consumed him entirely.

As he retreated to his room, I found myself grappling with my emotions. I watched him as he settled down at his computer, firing up Roblox, a world where he could escape into adventures and creativity. I hoped that the game would provide him with some solace, but I knew that the underlying issues remained unresolved.

Once the twins had settled down for their afternoon nap, I took a moment to gather my thoughts. The revelations of the day weighed heavily on my mind, and I realised that I needed to take action. Dylan needed more support than I could provide on my own.

I picked up my phone, my fingers trembling slightly as I scrolled through my contacts. I had been hesitant to seek outside help, fearing that it would label our family as broken. But the reality was clear: we were struggling, and I couldn't do it all on my own.

After a few moments of deliberation, I dialled the number for a local counselling service. My heart raced as the phone rang, and I felt a mix of anxiety and hope. I needed guidance, not just for Dylan but for the entire family. I wanted to create a space where we could talk about our feelings openly, where we could learn to process our grief together.

When a warm voice answered, I found myself spilling out the details of our situation, the challenges we faced, and the pain that had been simmering beneath the surface. "I think my son is struggling with the loss of his sister," I admitted, feeling the tears prick at the corners of my eyes. "And I'm scared that it's affecting him in ways I don't fully understand."

The counsellor listened patiently, offering words of reassurance and guidance. We discussed the importance of addressing Dylan's feelings, of helping him find healthy outlets for his anger and grief. I felt a sense of relief wash over me as we talked, as if a weight had been lifted.

After hanging up, I took a deep breath, feeling a renewed sense of purpose. I was determined to help Dylan, to guide him through his pain and help him find a way to heal.

As the afternoon wore on, I glanced at the door to Dylan's room, the sound of laughter and excitement emanating from his computer. I knew that he was still wrestling with his emotions, but I also hoped that he could find some solace in his games.

I resolved to check in on him later, to remind him that it was okay to feel what he was feeling, that he didn't have to carry the burden alone. Together, we would find a way to navigate the darkness, to honour Scarlett's memory while also embracing the love that surrounded us.

As the day wore on, I fell into my usual routine, darting between feeding the twins their bottles and playing with them, all while trying to get the house ready for the others to come home. The sun hung low in the sky, casting a warm glow through the windows, but inside, my mind was racing. I wanted everything to be perfect for everyone else, even as my own bruised nose throbbed with each movement.

I busied myself in the kitchen, chopping vegetables and stirring pots, the familiar sounds of dinner preparation providing a comforting backdrop to the chaos of my thoughts. The twins giggled as they reached for their toys, and I felt a small smile tugging at my lips as I watched them play. Their laughter was infectious, a sweet reminder of the joy amidst the struggles.

However, the worry about Dylan lingered in my mind. I knew I needed to address his feelings, his anger and grief over losing Scarlett. I hoped that the counselling would provide him with a safe space to express himself, to find a way to channel his emotions without lashing out.

Just as I was setting the table, I heard the front door open, and Ariel bounded in, her energy filling the room. "Mum! I'm home!" she called, her voice bright and cheerful. But as she caught sight of me, her expression shifted, concern etching itself onto her features. "What happened to your nose?"

I instinctively touched my face, feeling the bruised skin and dried blood beneath my fingers. "Oh, it's nothing, love. I just fell out of bed this morning when I went to make a cup of tea," I lied, forcing a smile, hoping to brush it off as inconsequential.

Ariel looked at me skeptically for a moment before surprising me with her response. "I bet it was Dylan!" she exclaimed, her eyes wide with a mix of accusation and amusement. Before I could respond, she dashed off to her room, leaving me standing there, a mixture of emotions swirling inside me.

I knew that Ariel had seen the chaos Dylan could create, but to hear her so casually suggest it stung. I tried to shrug it off, reminding myself that children often spoke without fully grasping the gravity of the situation.

Ariel was my little firecracker - a strong-willed 4-year-old with a personality that could light up a room. From the moment she burst into the world, her arrival had been a whirlwind. The traumatic birth left me shaken, but holding her tiny, squirming body in my arms, I knew she was a fighter. Ariel was my first child with Liam, and in those early months, we formed an unbreakable bond.

Then came Scarlett, my second child with Liam. She was Ariel's true sister, not half like the boys were, and over the 6 short months we had with her, the two girls grew inseparable. I'd watch Ariel dote on her baby sister, gently stroking Scarlett's soft cheek and singing her lullabies as Scarlett gazed up at her with wide, adoring eyes.

Ariel was the polar opposite of Scarlett in appearance. Her short, curly blonde hair framed a face marked by striking dark eyes that seemed to take in the world with an intensity beyond her years. Where Scarlett was the picture of grace and elegance, Ariel was all boundless energy and mischief.

Liam and I used to joke about how their personalities would play out as they got older. We'd imagine Ariel coming downstairs at midday, scratching her belly and asking what was for breakfast, while Scarlett would already be awake, her hair perfectly styled, reading a book and ready for lunch. Their contrasting natures were a constant source of amusement and wonder for us.

Of course, the future I had envisioned for those two girls would never come to pass. When Scarlett's life was tragically cut short at just 6 months old, a piece of my heart shattered beyond repair. The thought of Ariel growing up without her beloved sister, of never seeing the unique individuals they would have become - it was a sorrow too profound to fully express. In the wake of Scarlett's death, that vision of the feisty tomboy and the graceful princess faded, replaced by a deep, aching emptiness that threatened to swallow us whole. Ariel's laughter, once so carefree, now held a hint of melancholy, a subtle reminder of the sister she would never know.

As I finished preparing dinner, the warmth of the kitchen enveloped me, but I could feel the tension building again as the evening approached. Liam would be home soon, and I knew I needed to talk to him about the counselling.

When he finally walked through the door, his presence filled the space with a mix of relief and apprehension. "Hey, love," he said, dropping his bag by the door. "What's for dinner?"

"Just the usual," I replied, trying to keep my tone light. I knew I needed to approach the subject carefully. "I wanted to talk to you about something important regarding Dylan."

Liam raised an eyebrow, intrigued. "What is it?"

I took a deep breath, choosing my words carefully. "I've scheduled counselling for him. I think he needs a safe space to talk about everything he's feeling, especially after losing Scarlett."

He chuckled, shaking his head dismissively. "Counselling? Seriously? He'll just talk about his love for war and death and destruction like he always does. What good is that going to do?"

I felt a surge of frustration wash over me, but I kept my voice steady. "Liam, this isn't just about his interests. It's about helping him process his emotions, his anger, and his grief. He needs to know it's okay to feel what he's feeling."

"Fine, but I don't see how it's going to help," he replied, dismissing my concerns with a wave of his hand.

The conversation left a bitter taste in my mouth, but I didn't want to press further. Instead, I focused on dinner, the familiar routine of serving food providing a temporary distraction from the turmoil in my mind.

As night fell and we settled the twins into their cribs, I felt the exhaustion creeping in. I tucked them in, ensuring they were comfortable before heading to bed myself. But as I lay there, I found sleep elusive once again. I kept checking the twins, listening to their soft breaths, my mind racing with thoughts.

What would happen when I returned to work? I had wanted this job as a paramedic for years, pouring my heart into the training and the few months I had worked before becoming pregnant with the twins. But now, with Dylan's behaviour and the twins' needs, I couldn't shake the fear that I would struggle to balance it all.

During my pregnancy, I had often been called away from work to collect Dylan, who would act out in ways that required immediate attention. It wasn't just a matter of logistics; it felt like a constant battle of wills. I remembered those moments of panic when I'd receive a call from school, my heart racing as I dropped everything to rush to his side.

Liam had started off as Dylan's carer, but it had never felt right. I feared that if left alone with him, Dylan might change around Liam, that the anger he felt could manifest in ways that were harmful. I worried that Liam might flip, too, and the thought of them clashing sent chills down my spine.

As I lay in bed, the darkness of the night wrapping around me, I felt the weight of uncertainty settling in. My mind raced with the possibilities—what if I couldn't return to work? What if I couldn't manage the chaos of our family? The fear gnawed at me, but I pushed it aside, reminding myself that I was strong, that I had to be for my children.

With a deep breath, I resolved to face whatever came next, one day at a time. I would continue to fight for Dylan, to advocate for him and seek the support he needed. And perhaps, in doing so, I could also find a way to reclaim my own sense of self amidst the chaos.

As the clock struck 4:05 AM, exhaustion weighed heavily on my eyelids. I had just checked on the twins one last time, their soft breaths reassuring me in the dim light of the bedroom. The peaceful rhythm of their sleep wrapped around me like a warm blanket, but my mind raced with thoughts and memories.

I settled into bed, hoping for a few hours of rest. Just as I began to drift off, I felt an unfamiliar heaviness settle over me. Sleep paralysis gripped my body, rendering me unable to move. My heart raced as I sensed a presence in the room, shadows looming in the corners of my mind.

In the depths of this paralysis, a horrifying dream took shape. I found myself reliving a memory of my parents, a moment that filled me with dread. I watched helplessly as my father's anger erupted, and my mother's cries echoed in the silence. It was a scene of conflict and pain, a stark contrast to the peacefulness I had just witnessed in the twins.

The feeling of being trapped, both in my body and in that memory, was suffocating. I screamed silently, desperate to wake up, to escape the nightmare unfolding in my mind. Finally, with a rush of adrenaline, I broke free from the paralysis, gasping for breath as reality flooded back in.

The heaviness of the night lingered, but the warmth of the twins' presence brought me comfort. I closed my eyes once more, focusing on their soft breaths, and slowly let the darkness of sleep envelop me, hoping for a more peaceful dream this time.

As I lay there, hoping for a peaceful dream to wash away the remnants of the night, the comforting embrace of sleep never came. Instead, reality crashed in like a wave, pulling me from the depths of slumber. The soft sounds of the twins stirring in their cribs signalled the start of another chaotic day. It was 7 AM, and I knew it was time for their bottles.

Reluctantly, I nudged Liam awake, grateful he had a day off work to help. His presence was a lifeline in the manic whirlwind that had become our lives. As he stretched and blinked sleep from his eyes, I felt a mix of relief and gratitude. The day ahead would be a challenge, and having him by my side was a comfort amidst the chaos.

Life had become a confusing tapestry of emotions—love, grief, and the bittersweet pangs of parenting. As we moved through the morning routine, I watched Liam effortlessly prepare Dylan for school. It was a sight that stirred a complex blend of feelings within me. On one hand, I felt resentment for the ease with which he navigated the task, while on the other, I was filled with love for this young man who had embraced a difficult child that was not his own.

Dylan, with his relentless spiral of emotions, often overwhelmed me. I felt the weight of grief for our other children, who seemed lost in the chaos of our lives. The twins, while a joy, had also shifted the family dynamic in ways I couldn't fully grasp. The loss of our daughter still echoed in the corners of my heart, a reminder of the joy that had once filled our home, now overshadowed by the challenges we faced.

As I watched Liam help Dylan with his shoes, a sense of longing washed over me. The joy of parenting had become tangled in the complexities of our situation. It felt as though my other children were raising themselves amidst the turmoil, and I mourned the connection we once shared. I wanted to reach out to them, to guide them through the storm, but I often felt powerless against the tide of emotions that swirled around us.

The morning slipped away as we prepared for the day, each moment a reminder of the bittersweet reality we lived in. Love and resentment danced in my heart, a constant reminder of the complicated tapestry of our family life. And as we finally stepped out of the house, I made a silent promise to myself to find a way to reconnect with my children, to bring back the joy that seemed to have faded in the chaos of our lives.

When Liam returned home later that morning, the atmosphere felt heavy with unspoken worries. There were no phone calls from Dylan's school today to suggest he was having a good day, which left a knot of anxiety tightening in my stomach. I could see the concern etched on Liam's face as he suggested taking the twins out for a while so I could have some much-needed rest.

I hesitated, torn between the desire for a break and the nagging feeling that I should be doing something—anything—productive.

After a moment, I reluctantly agreed, knowing full well that I wouldn't truly rest. Instead, I would likely find something to clean, something to cook, or simply sit aimlessly scrolling through Facebook, losing myself in the lives of others while my own spiraled around me.

As Liam gathered the twins and prepared to leave, I felt a mix of gratitude and guilt wash over me. He was doing his best to help, but I couldn't shake the feeling that I should be the one managing everything. Once they were gone, the house fell into an eerie quiet, the kind that felt both peaceful and unnerving.

Ten minutes passed as I stood in the kitchen, waiting for the kettle to boil for a cup of tea. The sound of water bubbling filled the silence, and I attempted to gather my thoughts, trying to shake off the remnants of anxiety that clung to me.

Then, suddenly, there was a knock at the door. I froze, my heart racing instinctively. Who could it be? I hadn't been expecting anyone. With trepidation, I made my way to the door and opened it, only to be met by a figure that sent a chill down my spine.

There stood my father.

His presence filled the doorway, and before I could process the moment, he barged in forcefully, pushing me aside as if I were nothing more than a minor obstacle. I stumbled to the ground, shock coursing through me as I tried to regain my balance. Confusion and fear flooded my mind. Why was he here? What did he want?

I looked up at him, the man only a figure of dread. I felt the walls closing in around me, the chaos of my life suddenly swirling into a storm as I struggled to comprehend what was happening. This was not the way I had envisioned my day, and as I sat there on the floor, a sense of foreboding settled in—something dark and unsettling was about to unfold.

As my father locked the front door and pulled the curtains shut, an icy realization gripped me. I lay there frozen, my hand pressed against my head where it had banged against the floor quite violently. Pain throbbed through my skull, but it was nothing compared to the fear coursing through my veins.

"What do you want, Dad?" I managed to stammer, my voice trembling as I tried to mask the terror I felt.

His eyes blazed with fury as he stepped closer, and I could see the darkness that had always lurked beneath the surface now boiling over. "I want you dead, you bitch," he spat, his voice low and menacing. "Why did you tell Sienna what I had done to you and your sister? Sienna has only been part of my life for fucking moments, and you want to ruin my life like you always have. I will fucking kill you!"

The words hung heavy in the air, suffocating me with their weight. I wanted to scream, to fight back, but all I could do was stare up at him in disbelief. The memories of my childhood flooded back once again, moments of confusion, fear, and betrayal that I had desperately tried to bury every single day but never could.

Panic surged through me as I scrambled backward, my back pressing against the wall as I instinctively sought any semblance of safety. "Please, just leave!" I cried, my voice rising in pitch. "You don't have to do this!"

But he advanced, his rage palpable in the air. I could see the twisted mix of anger and desperation in his eyes, and it fuelled my own fight-or-flight response. I felt trapped, cornered in a room that suddenly felt like a prison.

In that moment, I knew I had to summon every ounce of strength within me. I couldn't let him take me down without a fight, I stand up. "You're the one ruining your life!" I shouted back, my voice trembling but defiant. "You think you can control me now as an adult after what I have fucking been through ? I won't let you!"

For a heartbeat, we stood there, locked in an unyielding stare, the silence thick with tension. Then, without warning, he lunged towards me, and instinct kicked in. I rolled to the side, narrowly avoiding his grasp. My heart raced as I scrambled to my feet, adrenaline surging through me.

I dashed for the kitchen, my mind racing for a way out. The back door! I could reach it if I could just get past him. I could hear his footsteps behind me, the sound echoing in my ears like a countdown.

As I reached the kitchen, I spotted a knife on the counter. I didn't want to use it, but desperation clawed at me. I grabbed it, my hands shaking as I turned to face him. "Stay back!" I shouted, brandishing the knife with a mixture of fear and determination.

His expression shifted, surprise mingling with fury. "You think you can scare me? You're nothing!" he growled, taking a step closer.

I took a shaky breath, my heart pounding as I realised this moment was pivotal. I could either let him overpower me or fight for my freedom. "Get out of my life!" I screamed, the words fuelled by years of pain, anger, and confusion.

For a moment, he hesitated, and in that split second, he looked scared.

As I stood there, knife in hand, I felt a surge of adrenaline overpower my fear. I couldn't let him control me any longer. With a quick breath, I charged at him, fuelled by a mix of desperation and defiance.

"Stay back!" I shouted, my voice echoing in the tense air as I lunged toward him. He reacted instinctively, moving to the side just as I aimed for his throat. My heart raced as I narrowly missed my target, the blade slicing through the air and plunging into the wall behind him with a sickening thud.

The impact reverberated through my hands, and I froze for a split second, the reality of what I had done crashing over me. My father's eyes widened in shock as he turned to face me, anger and disbelief etched across his features.

I quickly withdrew the knife from the wall, panic gripping me as I realised I had given him a moment to regain his composure. "You think you can get away with this?" he snarled, stepping closer, his fury igniting like a wildfire.

But something shifted within me. With every ounce of strength, I steadied myself, refusing to back down. "I will not let you hurt me anymore!" I shouted, my voice stronger than I felt.

He lunged, but I was ready this time. I sidestepped, using the momentum to my advantage as I aimed the knife toward him again. The fear that had once paralysed me now fuelled my determination to protect myself.

In that moment, I knew I had to fight back—not just for myself, but for the life I wanted to reclaim. The shadows of our past wouldn't dictate my future any longer. I was ready to face whatever came next, even if it meant standing against the very person who had once held such power over me. The chaos of our history would not dictate the outcome of this moment.

The air was thick with tension as I faced my father, the knife trembling in my grip. He glared at me, a mix of rage and disbelief in his eyes, but I could see a flicker of fear lurking beneath the surface. I had taken a stand, and it rattled him more than I had anticipated.

"Do you really think you can fight me?" he sneered, trying to mask his uncertainty. "You're still just a scared little girl."

In that moment, something within me snapped. I wasn't that scared girl anymore. I was a mother, a protector, and I had fought too hard to let him intimidate me. "I'm not afraid of you!" I shouted, filling my voice with the conviction I felt inside.

With renewed resolve, I lunged again, this time aiming lower. He sidestepped, but I was quicker, and I felt the blade graze his side as he stumbled back. A gasp escaped his lips, and for the first time, I saw a hint of vulnerability in his posture.

"Get away from me!" I yelled, pushing forward, my heart racing as adrenaline flooded my system. I could feel the fight coursing through me like a current, and I was determined not to let him take that away.

He brought his hand to his side, blood seeping through his fingers as panic washed over his face. "You're going to regret this," he hissed, but his bravado was faltering. He was no longer the imposing figure I remembered; he was just a man, vulnerable and desperate.

"Regret?" I shot back, my voice steady. "Regret is what you've brought into my life. You've haunted me for too long."

With each word, I felt the weight of years of pain begin to lift. This was a moment of empowerment, a chance to reclaim my narrative. I took a step closer, knife still poised, my breath steady despite the chaos around us.

"Leave," I commanded, my voice firm. "Get out of my life. You have no power over me anymore."

His eyes narrowed, fury igniting once more as he took a step toward me. But this time, I was ready. I raised the knife, my grip firm, and he halted in his tracks, the realisation of my determination dawning on him.

"Don't come any closer," I warned, my heart pounding in my chest. "I won't hesitate to defend myself."

For a moment, we stood there, locked in a battle of wills. I could see the gears turning in his mind, weighing his options as he assessed my resolve. Finally, with a snarl of frustration, he backed away, hands raised in mock surrender, but I knew better.

"Fine," he spat, his voice dripping with venom. "You think you've won? This isn't over."

With that, he turned and stormed out the back door, slamming it shut behind him. I stood there, breathless, the knife still clutched tightly in my hand. The silence that followed was deafening, filled with the echoes of what had just transpired.

As my heart slowly began to calm, I dropped the knife onto the table, my hands shaking. I felt a wave of emotions crash over me—relief, anger, and a deep-seated sorrow for the years lost. I had faced my father, and for the first time, I had not backed down.

But as I stood there in the aftermath, I knew that the battle was far from over. I would need to confront the scars of the past, not just for myself, but for my children. I would not let his darkness seep into their lives any longer.

Taking a deep breath, I gathered my thoughts. The chaos of the morning had been overwhelming, but I felt a flicker of hope igniting within me. I would seek help, I would find a way to heal, and I would protect my family at all costs.

As I moved to the window and peered outside, I knew the journey ahead would be challenging, but I was ready to face it head-on. I was reclaiming my life, and nothing would stand in my way again.

As I sat there, the adrenaline slowly fading, I couldn't shake the gnawing questions swirling in my mind. How had he found my home? Had he followed me that day I saw him at the train station, lurking in the shadows like a spectre? The thought sent a shiver down my spine; the reality of his presence felt suffocating. The walls of my own home, once a sanctuary, now felt like a cage.

I glanced towards the phone, the urge to call the police bubbling to the surface. But I hesitated, knowing that if I made that call, it would lead to more complications than answers. What would I say? That my father had barged into my home, threatening me with violence? The truth was, I was terrified of what the aftermath would bring. It wasn't just his wrath I feared; it was the possibility that both he and I could end up in trouble. I couldn't bear the thought of being dragged into a legal nightmare, not when I had my children to think about.

Instead, I reached for my phone, my heart pounding as I dialled Liam's number. I took a deep breath, steeling myself for the lie I was about to tell. "Come on, pick up," I whispered, anxiety prickling at my skin as the phone rang.

"Hey, love," Liam's voice finally came through, warm and welcoming, a stark contrast to the chaos swirling around me. "Everything alright?"

I paused, considering how to frame my response. "Um, not really," I said, forcing a casual tone that felt foreign. "I was wondering if you could pick up Dylan early from school today? I'm not feeling too great… flu-like symptoms, you know?"

I hated lying to him, but I felt I had no choice. I couldn't burden him with the truth; it would only add to the weight we were already carrying. I could sense his concern through the line, and it made my heart ache. "Of course, I can do that," he replied, his tone shifting to one of worry. "Do you need anything? Should I bring home some medicine?"

"No, no, I'll be fine," I rushed to say, trying to sound more convincing than I felt. "Just get Dylan, please."

"Alright, I'll be there as soon as I can," he said, and I could hear him moving around, likely gathering his things. "Just rest, yeah?"

"Yeah, I will," I replied, the knot in my stomach tightening as I ended the call. I felt a moment of relief wash over me, knowing that Liam would be home soon, but the underlying dread lingered.

I sank back into the chair, a wave of exhaustion washing over me. The chaos of the morning replayed in my mind like a film on loop—my father's threats, the fear that had gripped me so tightly. How could he have the audacity to waltz back into my life after everything?

As I sat there, I tried to focus on the mundane—what I would cook for dinner, how I would keep the twins entertained. But the weight of my father's visit loomed large, overshadowing every thought. Would he come back? Would he retaliate? The questions felt like a never-ending cycle, trapping me in a web of anxiety.

I glanced at the clock, time dragging painfully slow. Every minute felt like an eternity as I waited for Liam to return. I wanted to prepare myself, to act as if everything was normal when he walked through the door, but I knew that façade would shatter the moment he looked at me.

With each tick of the clock, I felt the urge to check the locks on the doors and windows, ensuring every barrier was secure. My heart raced at the thought of him finding a way back in. I could almost hear his voice in my head, taunting me, reminding me of the power he once held over me.

Eventually, the sound of the buggy wheels pulling up the drive grounded me. . Liam was here—thank goodness. I felt a rush of relief wash over me, but it was quickly followed by an overwhelming wave of dread. How was I going to explain the tension that hung thick in the air?

As he stepped through the front door, his expression shifted from concern to confusion. "Hey, love," he said, taking in my frazzled appearance. "You alright?"

I forced a smile, but I knew it didn't reach my eyes. "Just tired, really," I replied, my voice trembling slightly. "Dylan, go in the living room; I'll get some lunch ready!'

Liam beckoned Dylan out but kept his gaze on me, searching for something beneath the surface. I could feel his worry, like a weight pressing down on me, and I hated that I was putting him through this. But I was determined to keep the truth hidden, at least for now.

The tension in the air felt once again, suffocating and thick like heavy fog, a familiar vive . I needed to distract myself from the whirlwind of anxiety that threatened to consume me, and I remembered the twins were still in the buggy. Panic surged through me as I rushed over, suddenly fearing the worst. What if they'd been in there too long? What if something had happened to them? The irrational thought of them being dead, as it had crept in before, clawed at the edges of my mind.

As I reached the buggy, I quickly unfastened the straps, my hands shaking slightly in my haste. "Hey, my little ones!" I exclaimed, forcing a bright smile to mask my panic. They stirred, blinking sleepily up at me, their innocent faces bringing a moment of relief. I scooped them out, feeling the warmth of their tiny bodies against my chest.

"See? All fine," I muttered, though my heart was still racing. I turned back to the living room, only to find Liam standing there, arms crossed, a frown etched on his face.

"Back off, will you? Just go lay down for once," he said, his tone sharp. "I'll sort the twins and make lunch."

"No! I can't just sit there while you handle everything," I snapped, my frustration bubbling to the surface. "How do you think you can look after them when you were the one looking after Scarlett the day she died?"

His expression darkened, and for a moment, I regretted my words. But the anger felt justified; the guilt gnawed at me, and I couldn't help but lash out. "You think it's that easy for me? You think I've forgotten?"

"Yeah, well, you act like a heartless bitch sometimes!" he shot back, his voice rising in anger. "Maybe if you cared more about your family instead of spiralling into your own head, we wouldn't be in this mess!"

The words hit me like a slap, and I felt a wave of hurt wash over me. "Liam, I—"

But he was already walking out of the room, his expression one of pure frustration. I followed after him, desperation clawing at my throat. "I'm sorry, I didn't mean it like that!" I called, but he was already at the door.

"Just leave me out of it," he muttered, sticking his fingers up at me in a moment of sheer exasperation. The gesture felt like a dagger, and I felt the sting of tears prick at my eyes.

"Liam, please!" I pleaded, my heart racing as I reached for him. "I didn't mean what I said. I just—"

He turned to look at me, his eyes filled with hurt and anger. "You know what? I'm done," he spat, and with that, he stepped out of the house, slamming the door behind him.

I stood there, frozen, the silence that followed feeling deafening. The weight of everything crashed down on me—my father's threats, Liam's anger, the overwhelming sense of helplessness. The twins looked up at me, their innocent faces a stark reminder of the love that still existed amidst the chaos.

"Everything's going to be okay," I murmured to them, though I wasn't sure if I believed it myself. I felt like I was caught in a storm, battered by waves of guilt and fear. I sank onto the floor, cradling the twins in my arms, wishing I could shield them from the turmoil that had invaded our lives.

The evening crept in, the sun setting low on the horizon, casting long shadows through the house. Liam still has returned for the night. I have been waiting and and waiting, the clock ticking away the minutes, each second feeling heavier than the last. The sounds of the other children returning from school filled the air, their laughter and chatter a stark contrast to the turmoil inside me.

Dylan burst into everyone's bedrooms, a whirlwind of energy. He ran rampage around the house, excitement bubbling over, and I tried to match his weird enthusiasm, forcing a smile as I watched him. But my heart wasn't in it. I felt like I was going through the motions, trying to distract myself by making dinner and cleaning up the mess from earlier. I focused on chopping vegetables, the rhythmic sound of the knife against the cutting board grounding me, but it wasn't enough to erase the gnawing worry in my chest.

I reached for my phone, the urge to call Liam overwhelming. I needed to hear his voice, to know that he was okay. But when I dialled, the call went straight to voicemail. Panic set in as I realised his phone was off. "Please, Liam," I whispered, my heart racing. "Just come home."

Fear gripped me, a suffocating weight. What if he never came back? Or worse, what if he went and slept with someone else? The thought was a bitter pill to swallow, dredging up memories I had tried so hard to forget. Years ago, we had argued, and that's exactly what he had done. I remembered the nights I'd spent in despair, knowing he was out there, messaging girls for sex, looking at their naked bodies on the computer, and eventually meeting up with a couple. I had found out one time by using his phone, the images flickering across the screen like taunts.

Even though Liam was my world, the pain of that betrayal had cut deep. I had thought we were past all of that, that he had changed, but now doubts crept in. I couldn't shake the feeling that he might be seeking revenge, that my words had pushed him back into the arms of someone else.

As I stirred the sauce on the stove, I felt tears prick at my eyes. I had wanted to hurt him, to make him understand the gravity of my fears, but now I was left with the haunting realisation that I might have driven him away for good. The memories of our past loomed large, a shadow that threatened to swallow me whole.

"Come on, Bea, pull yourself together," I muttered under my breath, trying to focus on the present. I glanced over at the twins, who were happily playing with their toys, their innocence a stark reminder of all I had to protect. I couldn't let my fears consume me; I had to keep it together for their sake.

Dylan came bouncing into the kitchen, his face flushed with excitement. "Mum, can we have pasta for dinner?" he asked, his eyes shining with anticipation.

"Of course, sweetheart," I replied, forcing a smile. "Pasta it is." I added the noodles to the boiling water, trying to push the worry aside, but it lingered like a dark cloud overhead.

As the evening wore on, the house grew quiet. I set the table, my mind racing with thoughts of Liam. I replayed the last conversation in my head, wishing I could take back my words, wishing I could hold him and make everything right again. But the longer he stayed away, the more I felt the distance between us grow.

With dinner ready, I called the children to the table, but the joy of the moment was overshadowed by the absence of Liam. As we sat down to eat, I glanced at the empty chair across from me, my heart aching. I tried to engage the kids, to make it feel normal, but the laughter felt hollow without Liam's presence.

After dinner, I cleaned up in a daze, the weight of uncertainty pressing down on me. I wanted to believe he would come home, that he would walk through the door with an apologetic smile, but deep down, fear gnawed at me. I couldn't help but wonder if I was losing him all over again.

As the night wore on, I tucked the twins into bed, their soft breaths a soothing reminder of the love that still existed amidst the chaos. I lingered for a moment.

Finally, I made my way to the living room, the silence settling around me like a heavy blanket. I picked up my phone again, staring at it as if it would somehow magically ring with news of Liam. But nothing came. I sank onto the sofa, my heart heavy, the shadows of the past creeping back in.

I knew I had to confront my fears, to face the possibility that I might have pushed him away for good. But more than anything, I had to hold onto hope. Hope that he would return, that we could mend what had been broken, and that we could move forward together, stronger than before.

As the familiar alarm of the twins blared at 7am, the shrill sound cut through the stillness of the house like a knife. I dragged myself out of bed, my heart heavy with lingering anxiety from the day before. The sound filled the air, mingling with the soft rustling of the children as they stirred from their slumber. I shuffled into the kitchen, the cool tiles beneath my feet sending a shiver up my spine, and began to prepare their bottles as per usual. Yet, today felt different.

A strange sense of fear gripped me as I stood alone in the kitchen, the silence amplifying the unease swirling in my gut. All the other children were asleep, blissfully unaware of the tension that seemed to cling to the air like fog. Liam wasn't home—his absence was palpable. I glanced over at the shoe cabinet, expecting to see his familiar trainers tossed carelessly on top, a habit I often chastised him for. He never bothered to put them inside the cabinet, a small mess that irked me to no end. I liked order; I craved cleanliness. But Liam? He was indifferent to it all, as if chaos didn't bother him, even if it were on fire.

As I shook the twins' baby bottles, staring out of the window, I couldn't shake the feeling that I wasn't alone in this room. It was as if the shadows had taken on a life of their own, creeping in around me. Perhaps it was just my mind playing tricks, a remnant of the chaos from yesterday when my father had barged in, throwing my world off balance. The memories of his presence lingered, and the nausea it brought churned in my stomach. I felt trapped, like a moth drawn to a flame, tethered to the darkness of my past.

Hoping to catch a glimpse of Liam's red hair as he made his way back home, I kept my gaze fixed on the street outside. But instead of the reassurance of his familiar figure, I was met with an unexpected force to the back of my head, something more powerful than the morning light spilling through the window. I don't know what had hit me at this point. My heart raced as I turned, my mind racing through a thousand scenarios, thinking it might be Dylan, already testing his boundaries, ready to unleash his antics on me at this early hour.

But when I turned around, my breath caught in my throat. It wasn't Dylan. It was my father.

The shock hit me like a cold wave, freezing me in place. "How did you get in?" I gasped, panic surging through my veins. I had locked the door last night; I was certain of it. My heart pounded as I took a step back, instinctively protecting the twins, who were blissfully unaware of the danger lurking in our home.

He stood there, a menacing figure framed by the doorway, his presence suffocating the very air around me. The familiar scent of cigarettes and something darker clung to him, a reminder of the man I had tried so hard to escape. My pulse quickened as dread washed over me, flooding my senses. I felt as if the ground beneath me had vanished, leaving me teetering on the edge of a precipice.

"What are you doing here?" I demanded, my voice trembling despite my effort to sound strong. I could feel the bile rising in my throat as I fought to maintain control over my emotions. The twins were still in their playpen, oblivious to the storm that was about to unfold. I don't know what he had hit me with but my head hurts.

"I came to see you, Bea," he replied, his voice low and gravelly, laced with an unsettling calmness that made my skin crawl. "We need to talk."

Panic erupted within me, a primal instinct to protect my children taking precedence over everything else. "Get out," I said, my voice barely above a whisper, yet firm. I didn't want him here; I didn't want him to have any part in my life. I had fought too hard to escape his grasp, to carve out a semblance of safety for my family.

But he stepped forward, a predator closing in on its prey. "You can't keep me out forever, Bea. I'm your father," he sneered, and I could see the darkness swirling in his eyes, a reminder of the pain he had inflicted on me in the past.

Every instinct screamed at me to run, to escape, but I was rooted to the spot, fear anchoring me. The walls of the kitchen seemed to close in, the weight of his presence suffocating. I felt the urge to scream, to call for help, but I couldn't risk putting the twins in danger.

As I stood there, the reality of the moment crashed down on me. This was the man who had haunted my childhood, the embodiment of my deepest fears. I had thought I was safe, that I had built a life free from his torment, aside from the flashbacks, but here he was, tearing down the walls I had so carefully constructed.

"Stay away from my children!" I shouted, a surge of defiance igniting within me. I had to protect them at all costs. The twins at this moment were my priority; I wouldn't let him disrupt their innocence. Just like he had mine.

For a moment, he hesitated, a flicker of uncertainty crossing his face, but it quickly vanished. "You don't get to dictate anything, Bea," he said, stepping closer, the menace in his tone unmistakable. "I'm still your father, and you need to remember that."

I felt my heart race, the fight-or-flight instinct kicking in. I had to stand my ground. "I don't need you," I spat, forcing myself to remain calm even as the tremors of fear coursed through me. "You're not welcome here, I told you yesterday! Why can't you just leave me alone!'

With each word, I felt the strength of my resolve grow. I wouldn't let him take away what I had built. I wouldn't let him shatter the fragile peace I had fought so hard to establish.

But as he moved closer, I realised that this confrontation was far from over. The battle for my life, for my children, had only just begun. And I was determined to win.

As the tension in the kitchen thickened, Dylan suddenly appears in the doorway, rubbing the sleep from his eyes. He looked between me and my father, confusion etched on his innocent face. "Mum, who's this man?" he asked, his tone curious rather than fearful.

My heart sank as I realised how easily he could be drawn into this nightmare. I glanced at my father, who immediately shifted his demeanour, the menace in his eyes replaced by a façade of charm. It was as if a switch had flipped, and the predator had morphed into a fun-loving character, reminiscent of a gift of the gab salesman from that old sitcom we used to watch.

"I'm your granddad, mate!" he exclaimed, flashing a grin that didn't quite reach his eyes. "I've come to visit you and your lovely mum. I've got some exciting stories to tell!"

Dylan's face lit up, the thrill of meeting someone new eclipsing any sense of caution. He loved new people, always eager to make friends and bring joy into the mundane. "Really? Granddad?" he repeated, his eyes sparkling with enthusiasm. "Can you come see my room? I've got toys and everything!"

Before I could intervene, Dylan bounded across the kitchen, his hand reaching for my father's. "Come on, I'll show you!" he chirped, completely oblivious to the danger that lingered in the air.

I wanted to scream. "Dylan, no! Don't—" But the words caught in my throat as dread crashed over me. My father's smile widened as he followed Dylan, feigning warmth and excitement while I felt my heart race with panic.

"Lead the way, little man!" he said, playing the part of the doting grandfather, a role he had never truly embraced because I wouldn't allow it . I could see the twisted joy in his eyes, relishing the idea of being welcomed into my son's world, a world I had fought so hard to protect.

Dylan, with his PDA and nine-year-old body but a two-year-old mind, had no sense of the danger that lurked behind my father's charm. He had never been taught to fear strangers; I had always believed in the goodness of people, even when my own father had proved otherwise. It was a lesson I had learned too late, and now it felt like a cruel joke.

"Dylan, wait!" I shouted, my voice trembling with urgency. But it was too late; they had already disappeared down the hallway, my father's laughter echoing in my ears like a dark omen.

I felt the walls of the kitchen closing in on me again, my breath coming in shallow gasps. Panic surged within me as I raced after them, my heart pounding in my chest. What was he doing with my son? What kind of game was he playing?

As I reached the entrance to the hallway, I could see Dylan eagerly showing my father around his room, pointing to his toys with unabashed excitement. The sight made my blood run cold. "This is my favourite train!" he exclaimed, completely unaware of the danger that loomed just a few steps away.

"Very impressive, mate," my father replied, kneeling down to inspect the toy, his voice dripping with feigned enthusiasm. "You've got quite the collection here!"

"Do you want to play with me?" Dylan asked, his innocent hope shining through. The words struck me like a slap, and I felt a wave of nausea wash over me. I couldn't let this happen; I couldn't allow my father to infiltrate our lives again, especially not now.

"Dylan, come back to me!" I called, my voice breaking. "Please!"

My father looked up at me, a smug grin plastered on his face. "Let's just have a little fun, Bea. I'm family, after all," he said, his tone patronising, as if I were overreacting, as if he had every right to be there.

"Family?" I spat, stepping forward, my protective instincts flaring. "You're not family! Not after everything you've done!"

Dylan glanced between us, confusion clouding his features. "Mum, what's wrong?" he asked, his enthusiasm fading as he sensed the tension in the air.

I rushed to my son's side, kneeling to his level, forcing myself to meet his gaze. "Listen to me, sweetheart. I need you to come with me right now, okay? We're going to play in the living room. Just you and me."

His brow furrowed, uncertainty creeping in. "But I want to show Granddad my trains!"

"No!" I said, the desperation in my voice rising. "You don't understand. He's not safe. We need to go, now!"

My father rose to his feet, an ominous shadow looming behind me. "Come on, Bea. Don't be ridiculous. I'm just trying to bond with my grandson. Let him enjoy his childhood."

"No!" I shouted, turning to face him, adrenaline coursing through my veins. "You lost that right a long time ago. You're not welcome here!"

Dylan looked between us, confusion and fear flickering in his eyes, and I felt my heart ache for him. I couldn't let my father manipulate him; I couldn't let him take away the innocence that still remained.

"Dylan, come with me," I pleaded, reaching for his hand. "Now."

With a hesitant glance at my father, Dylan finally took my hand, and I felt a rush of relief mixed with lingering dread. I had to get us out of that room, away from the danger that threatened to engulf us.

As we turned to leave, I could feel my father's gaze burning into my back, the tension crackling in the air. "You can't keep me away forever, Bea," he called after us, his voice laced with menace. "I'll always be watching."

I swallowed hard, determination flooding my veins. I wouldn't let him win. I would protect my children, no matter the cost.

Just as I settled Dylan on the couch, trying to distract him with a favourite cartoon, the sound of footsteps echoed through the house. One by one, the other children began to wake, their groggy bodies stumbling into the living room as the reality of another school day loomed ahead.

Jax, my eldest, stepped into the room, his brow furrowed with concern. His protective instincts kicked in immediately as he sensed the tension in the air. "Mum, what's going on?" he asked, glancing from me to my father, who was trying his best to engage Dylan in a game of pretend.

"Everything's fine, love," I said, forcing a smile, though my heart raced. I could see the worry etched on Jax's face, and I knew he wasn't convinced. He moved closer, beckoning Harley and Ariel back toward their rooms. "Come on, you two, back to your rooms for a bit," he instructed, his tone firm yet gentle.

As they shuffled away, Jax turned back to me, a glimmer of mischief flashing in his eyes. "I think it's a day off school today, don't you, Mum?" he said, his voice light, as if trying to lighten the mood. Then, without waiting for a response, he rushed off, leaving me feeling more isolated than ever.

Just then, the front door creaked open, and I felt a rush of hope. Liam was home. I turned to greet him, but my heart sank as I saw the look on his face. He froze in the doorway, his eyes narrowing as he took in the scene. Dylan sat on the floor, laughing and playing with my father, who wore a manic grin that sent chills down my spine.

"Bea? What the hell is going on?" Liam's voice was low but edged with fury as he stepped further into the room. He noticed the blood at the back of my head, likely from the impact earlier, and his expression darkened. "What happened to you?"

"It's nothing," I stammered, but I could see the concern in his eyes turning to rage as he turned his attention to my father.

"What the hell is this?" he demanded, stepping closer, a growl low in his throat.

"Just a friendly visit, Liam," my father chirped, his tone dripping with false cheerfulness. "Dylan and I were just getting to know each other better!"

"Dylan!" Liam shouted, and my son jumped, turning to look at him wide-eyed. "Come here right now!"

Dylan's innocent excitement faded as he hopped up, confusion clouding his features. "But, Liam, I was—"

"Now!" Liam's command cut through the air, and Dylan hurried over to him, seeking comfort.

Liam's gaze shifted back to my father, who was still grinning with that unnerving, almost childlike enthusiasm. "You think you can just waltz in here and play happy families?" he spat, his voice rising. "You're nothing but a dirty pedophile and a monster! You don't belong here!"

"Oh, Liam, is that any way to speak to your father in law?" my father retorted, his laughter echoing in the room, almost resembling Dylan's when he was overexcited. "I'm just trying to be a part of your kids life. Isn't that what you want?"

"Get away from him!" Liam shouted again, anger radiating off him as he moved towards the kitchen. I felt a flicker of fear, knowing he was about to arm himself.

I watched as he opened the kitchen drawer, his hands shaking slightly as he pulled out a knife—the blade glinting menacingly in the light. It was a chef's knife, long and sleek, with a sharp edge that seemed to reflect the turmoil brewing within him. The handle was made of polished wood, smooth and sturdy, fitting perfectly in his grip. I knew he'd used it countless times to prepare our meals, but now it would serve a far more sinister purpose.

"Liam, please!" I cried, panic rising in my chest as I rushed to stop him. "Don't!"

But my father merely laughed, a sound that sent chills down my spine. "What's he going to do with that, Bea? Slice a cucumber? You think that scares me?" His voice dripped with mockery, and I could see the madness behind his eyes.

"Get away from my son!" Liam shouted, brandishing the knife, his expression fierce. "You have no right to be here. You think you can just walk back into our lives like nothing happened?"

"Oh, but I have every right," my father sneered, stepping forward, undeterred by the weapon. "You're the one who's been keeping them from me. I'm family, Liam. You're just a pathetic excuse for a father."

"Family? You're nothing to us!" Liam spat, his voice full of fury as he moved closer, the knife glinting ominously in the light. "You're a monster, and I'll make sure you never come near my kids again."

My father took a step closer, his bravado unshaken. "You think you can scare me with that little knife? Look at you, all worked up. It's amusing, really. But you should know something—I've been through worse."

I felt the tension in the room crackle like electricity. The air was thick with hostility, and I could feel the panic rising within me. "Liam, don't!" I pleaded, desperate to defuse the situation. "He's not worth it!"

But Liam's eyes were locked onto my father, a storm of emotions swirling within him. "You don't get to threaten my family anymore," he said, his voice low and steady.

"Threaten?" my father chuckled darkly. "I'm not the one with the knife, am I? You're the one who should be scared."

As the words hung in the air, I felt the weight of the moment pressing down on me. The tension was palpable, and I knew that everything could change in an instant. It was a standoff, a battle of wills that threatened to spiral out of control.

"Liam, please," I begged, my heart racing. "We need to think about the kids."

"Stay out of this, Bea!" he snapped, his gaze never leaving my father.

"Why don't we all just take a step back?" my father suggested, his tone deceptively calm. "Dylan just wants to have fun. Isn't that right, son?"

Dylan, caught in the crossfire, looked between the three of us, confusion and fear flickering in his eyes. "Liam? Mum? What's going on?"

"No, no, no!" I exclaimed, rushing to Dylan's side. "Everything's going to be fine, sweetheart. Just a misunderstanding."

"Misunderstanding?" Liam echoed, his voice low and dangerous. "You think this is a misunderstanding? This is a monster in our home, and I'm not going to let him take anything away from you again!"

The tension reached a boiling point, and I felt the world around me teetering on the edge. I had to find a way to protect my family, to keep the darkness at bay. But as I stood there, caught in the storm, I knew that the battle was far from over.

The tension in the room thickened as my father leaned back, a smug grin playing on his lips. "You know, I heard from your mother about Scarlett," he said, his voice dripping with condescension. "Such a tragedy, really. But we both know it was your fault, wasn't it? Leaving a six-month-old sleeping in a room with the door closed. What did you think would happen?"

Liam's face turned crimson, his fists clenching around the knife as his fury bubbled to the surface. "You don't get to talk about her!

You shut your mouth right now, or I swear I will end you right here!" His voice was low and menacing, filled with rage that radiated through the room.

Dylan, caught up in the whirlwind of emotions, giggled at the escalating tension. "Do it, Liam!" he shouted, his excitement bubbling over as he began to stim, bouncing on his toes, his little hands flapping in a rhythm only he understood. "Do it! Do it!"

"Dylan, stop!" I cried, panic surging through me. This wasn't a game; this was real, and I needed to keep my son safe. My heart raced as I glanced at Liam, whose expression was a volatile mix of anger and desperation.

"Liam, don't listen to him!" I shouted, my voice rising above the chaos. "He's a nasty monster! He ruined my life! I wanted to protect my own messed-up family, but I should've got him arrested years ago!"

My father smirked, clearly revelling in the turmoil he was causing. "Ah, Bea, such melodrama. It's almost entertaining. But let's be honest; you're just as much a part of this mess as I am."

"Shut up!" Liam thundered, taking a step forward, the knife still clutched tightly in his hand. "You don't get to turn this around on her! You're the one who's sick! You're the one who's been a danger to this family!"

"Oh, I'm a danger? Look at you, waving a knife around like a child playing with a toy! You're pathetic, Liam. You think you're some kind of protector?" my father taunted, his laughter ringing hollow and chilling.

"Liam, please!" I shouted, desperation creeping into my voice. "You don't need to sink to his level! You're better than this! We can handle this another way!"

But Liam's eyes were wild, consumed by rage. "He deserves to feel fear! He deserves to know what it's like to be threatened for once in his life!" He took another step closer, and my heart raced, terrified of what might happen next.

"Do it, Liam!" Dylan shouted again, his laughter echoing in stark contrast to the tension surrounding us. "Make him go away!"

"Dylan, no!" I yelled, moving closer to my son, trying to shield him from the chaos. "This isn't a game! This is serious!"

The argument reached a fever pitch, and just then, the sound of sirens pierced through the air, slicing through the tension like a knife. A cold wave of realisation washed over me. "Who called the police?" I gasped, my heart racing. The shrill wail of sirens grew louder, echoing down the street. Had the neighbours heard us screaming? Did they know what was happening in our home?

"Great, just great!" my father sneered, his bravado faltering slightly. "You think they'll believe you? After all the things you've done? They'll just think you're the crazy one!"

Liam's expression hardened, the anger still burning in his eyes. "I don't care what they think! I just want you out of my life for good!" He turned to me, the knife still gripped tightly in his hand. "We can end this, Bea. Just say the word."

"Liam, please!" I pleaded, my voice breaking. "This isn't the way! We need to keep the kids safe! They can't see this!"

The sirens grew closer, and I could hear the faint sounds of shouting outside, voices rising above the chaos. I glanced at Dylan, who was still giggling, oblivious to the gravity of the situation. My heart sank as I thought of the twins, still crying in their playpen, yearning for their morning bottles.

"Dylan, you need to listen to me!" I urged, kneeling down to his level. "This is not a game. We need to go somewhere safe!"

"Safe?" my father mocked. "You think running away will protect you? You're just a bunch of scared little rabbits. You don't know what real danger is."

"Shut up!" Liam shouted, his voice echoing through the room. "You're nothing but a coward hiding behind your twisted words!"

The sound of sirens reached a crescendo, and I felt the walls closing in around me. I needed to find a way to protect my family—before it was too late. The reality of the situation crashed down on me, and I knew that this confrontation was going to cause a lot of problems for all of us, even more so than anything we've ever been through

As the tension in the room reached a boiling point, the police had arrived in full force. Without hesitation, they slammed down the door, the wood splintering under the impact.

"Police! Hands up!" one officer shouted, his voice cutting through the chaos. The sight that greeted them was a scene of turmoil—Liam stood in the middle of the room, a knife clutched tightly in his hand, eyes wide with a mix of fear and defiance.

In stark contrast, my father took on a façade of victimhood, his hands raised in a pleading gesture. "I didn't do anything! He's the one you want!" he cried out, his voice dripping with desperation as he pointed a shaking finger at Liam. The officers assessed the situation quickly. They instinctively moved between the two, ready to step in.

"Drop the weapon!" another officer commanded, moving forward with caution. The air was thick with tension, and Liam's grip on the knife faltered for a moment as he glanced between the officers and my father, confusion clouding his judgment.

"Liam, just put it down," I urged, hoping to reach him through the chaos. But my father's theatrics only intensified. "You have to listen to the police, Liam! You'll get hurt!" he shouted, his voice echoing in the charged atmosphere.

The officers moved in swiftly, their training kicking in as they worked to de-escalate the situation. One officer stepped closer to Liam, speaking in a calm, steady tone, "Let's talk about this. You don't need to hurt anyone. Just put the knife down, and we can help you."

The scene was a whirlwind of emotions—fear, betrayal, and a desperate need for resolution. Liam's eyes darted around, the weight of the moment pressing down on him as the police continued their attempt to diffuse the situation.

The tension continued to hang heavy in the air as Liam's fingers slowly loosened their grip on the knife. The blade clattered to the floor, echoing like a gunshot in the stunned silence that followed. He looked around, confusion and fear swirling in his eyes, as the officers quickly moved in to secure him.

"Good job, Liam," one of the officers said, a hint of relief in his voice. My father was still playing his part, his expression a mask of innocence. "All he did was try to attack me while I was just trying to see my grandchildren!" he exclaimed, his voice rising dramatically. "You have to understand, I was merely trying to be a good grandfather! He's the one who's gone mad!"

Dylan, standing off to the side, bounced on his heels, his wide eyes sparkling with excitement at the sight of the officers. "Look, Mum! The police are here! This is so cool!" he shouted, oblivious to the gravity of the situation. "I wanna be a police officer when I grow up! Get on the ground now!" he yelled, mimicking the commands he had seen in films, his small voice filled with enthusiasm.

One of the female officers knelt down to Dylan's level, a warm smile on her face despite the chaos surrounding them. "Hey there, mate. How about we step outside for a moment? I'd love to have a chat with you," she said gently, sensing a need to remove him from the turmoil inside.

As she took his hand, leading him away, a wave of dread washed over me. What if Dylan's enthusiasm caught the wrong attention? What if his innocent demeanour, paired with the scene unfolding, led to questions that could open doors to further trouble? Anxiety clenched my chest as I watched them disappear outside, leaving me alone with the aftermath of the chaos.

How had life spiralled to this point? My mind raced as I reflected on the series of events that had brought us here—my father's manipulative patterns, Liam's descent into turmoil, and now the police intervention that felt like a shattering of what little stability we had left.

I glanced at Liam, now being handcuffed by the officers, his eyes filled with regret. The room felt suffocating, the walls closing in again as I grappled with the reality of our lives. Memories of happier times flickered through my mind like an old stop motion movie, starkly contrasting the chaos now surrounding us. How had it come to this?

The world outside felt distant, as if we were trapped in a nightmare with no way out. All I could think about was the weight of this moment and how it would linger in our lives—a haunting reminder of the choices made and the innocence lost.

As the chaos unfolded, a sudden surge of urgency propelled me forward. I couldn't let Liam be taken away like this. I dashed past the officers, leaving the crying twins still unsettled in their playpen, their little faces scrunched up in confusion. The other children remained in the room with Jax, blissfully unaware of the turmoil that had erupted in their home.

"Liam!" I shouted, my voice cracking as I ran after him. The officers were leading him towards the front door, and I could feel my heart pounding in my chest. "Wait! Please, just wait!"

He turned slightly, his eyes reflecting a mix of fear and despair. "I didn't mean for any of this to happen," he said, his voice barely above a whisper.

"Liam, listen to me!" I pleaded, my desperation spilling out. "You're not the one who should be arrested! It's my father—the real monster is him! He's the one who's hurt me! He's the one who needs to face the consequences of his actions!"

The officers paused, looking at me with a mixture of confusion and concern. I seized the moment, stepping closer, my voice rising with urgency. "You don't understand! For years, he's hidden behind a façade of innocence while he's inflicted pain on me, manipulating me into silence! He's the one who has abused trust and caused a lifetime of trauma!"

The gravity of my words hung in the air, and I could see the officers exchanging glances, weighing the situation. "Please," I continued, my heart racing. "You have to believe me. Liam is just a victim in all of this—he's been pushed to the edge by my father's cruelty. He's not a criminal; he's a survivor! We need to stop this cycle of abuse before it destroys any more lives!"

The weight of my plea settled in the room, and for a moment, I felt a glimmer of hope. I had to make them see the truth, to understand that the real threat lay not in Liam's actions but in the past that haunted me.

"Think about it," I implored, my voice steadying. "If you arrest Liam, it will only give my father the chance to continue his reign of terror. He must be held accountable for what he's done. We can't let him win."

The officers exchanged looks again, and I could sense the shift in their stance. I felt a flicker of possibility, a chance to reclaim our narrative. The fight for justice had begun, and I was determined to see it through, to protect those I loved and bring the true monster to light.

The officers exchanged glances, their expressions a mixture of sympathy and resolve. "Listen, we have a duty to arrest Liam," one of them said gently, yet firmly. "He was wielding a weapon, and we can't overlook that. But we understand this is complicated. We'll have one of our officers come into the house to interview you about what's been happening."

My heart dropped as they continued. "However, given the situation with the children present, we'll need to call social services to come and remove them until this is resolved. It's for their safety."

The words felt like a punch to the chest, knocking the breath out of me. My mind spiralled as I recalled the agony of losing baby Scarlett, the emptiness that had consumed me since that day. The thought of losing my other children, even temporarily, was unbearable. "No, please," I gasped, my voice trembling as panic began to set in. "Not them! I can't lose them too!"

The officers looked at me with concern, but their duty was clear. I felt the world closing in around me, the walls of the room tightening like a vice. My breath quickened, and I could feel the familiar grip of a panic attack taking hold. I fought against it, but the darkness began to seep in, swallowing me whole.

"Stay with us," one of the officers urged, but the words faded into a distant echo as I felt myself slipping away. The room blurred, and I collapsed, the last thing I remembered being the cold floor beneath me.

When I awoke, the harsh fluorescent lights of the hospital were glaring above me, and the sterile smell of antiseptic filled my nostrils. Panic surged through me again as reality rushed back—where were my children? Had they really taken them?

I bolted upright, my heart racing as I scanned the room, searching for familiar faces. A nurse rushed in, her expression calm but concerned. "Easy now, love. You've had quite a scare," she said gently, placing a hand on my shoulder. "You're safe here."

"Where are my children?" I demanded, my voice raw and frantic. "Are they okay? Did social services take them?"

The nurse hesitated, her expression softening. "They're safe. Social services are involved, but you'll have a chance to see them soon. Just take a deep breath for me."

But it felt impossible to breathe. My mind raced with thoughts of loss and fear. The shadows of my past loomed large, threatening to engulf me again. I couldn't bear the thought of being separated from my children, not when I had fought so hard to keep them safe.

As the nurse continued to speak, her voice a soothing balm against my rising panic, I realised that this fight was far from over. I needed to reclaim my strength, to stand up against the darkness that threatened to consume us all. The road ahead would be difficult, but I had to find a way to protect my children and confront the monsters in our lives, because that's all I have ever done for years and years. I don't care about me, just them.

As I sat staring at the stark hospital wall with, the beeping machines, I felt a sense of despair wash over me. A drip hung from my arm, tethering me to this place, while my children were somewhere else, and Liam was arrested, God knows where. My father was likely still plotting his next move I'm sure of it , hidden away from the chaos he had caused.

I pressed the button to summon another nurse, feeling the weight of my situation pressing down on me. A moment later, the door swung open, and in walked a nurse who was striking yet stern, her mixed-race features framed by beautifully styled blonde hair. Her beauty was overshadowed by her abruptness as she approached my bedside.

"What do you need?" she asked, her tone clipped and businesslike.

"When can I go home?" I asked, my voice trembling. "I feel much better now. I need to get back to my children and Liam."

"It's not my decision," she replied, barely glancing at me. "The doctor will be around in the morning."

A wave of fear washed over me. I hated hospitals, and the thought of spending another night here sent a surge of rage through me. "I can't stay here!" I shouted, feeling the panic rise within me. "I need to be with my children!"

"Calm down," she said, her voice steady but lacking empathy.

But I couldn't calm down. The fear, the overwhelming anxiety, took control. In a moment of desperation, I ripped the drip from my arm, the movement sharp and reckless. Without a second thought, I bolted from the bed, dressed only in a flimsy hospital gown, shoeless and vulnerable. The cold floor beneath my feet reminded me of that day—the day I lost Scarlett.

That day was etched in my memory, a haunting reminder of my worst fears realised. It was my first day back at work after Scarlett was born. I called Liam to check on her while he played Xbox with Ariel. I asked him to go upstairs and see Scarlett. I felt a nagging worry, but I brushed it aside.

When Liam took the phone and Ariel, time felt like it stopped. I remember the wild screams that cut through the air, then the sound of the phone dropping. My heart sank, and a cold dread settled in my stomach. I knew something was wrong with Scarlett, but I tried to convince myself that I was being overdramatic. Surely, everything was fine.

I had run out of the building where I worked, not saying a word to anyone as I dashed into the street, begging a car to stop. I needed to get home. In the car, I called the ambulance and the police, just in case something tragic had happened. I kept telling myself I was being stupid, that everything would be alright, but deep down, I felt the darkness creeping in.

When I finally arrived home, I kicked my shoes off, adrenaline propelling me up the stairs. I found Ariel still playing in the hallway, blissfully unaware of the storm that had just hit our family. But then I saw Liam, crouched over Scarlett's body, a phone by his side, the operator screaming out CPR instructions.

The image was seared into my mind—the sight of him desperately trying to save her, the futility of it all. The screams, the panic, the overwhelming sense of loss—it all rushed back to me now as I stood shoeless in the hospital, fear coursing through my veins. I had to get out of here. I had to get my children back.

With a surge of determination, I dash through the hospital corridors, the sterile air now suffocating.

I bolted out of the hospital, my heart racing with each step. The world outside was a blur, but I didn't stop to take it in. I needed to get home. I needed to see my children, to feel their warmth, to reassure myself that they were alright.

As I stumbled onto the street, I flagged down a taxi. The driver, a middle-aged man with a scruffy beard and a bemused expression, raised an eyebrow at my hospital gown.

"Where to, love?" he asked, his voice laced with concern.

"Just drive! Please, I need to get home," I urged, my voice trembling with urgency.

"Alright then, hold tight," he replied, pulling away from the curb.

I could feel his gaze in the rear-view mirror, a mix of confusion and sympathy. "You alright? You look a bit... shaken."

"I just need to make a few calls," I said, my mind racing. "I need to get my children back. I can't be away from them, not again."

He nodded, obviously unsure of what to say but willing to help. "We'll get you home in a jiffy. Just hang in there."

As the taxi sped through the streets, I tried to push the thoughts of what might await me at home out of my mind. What if my father was there? What if the police were still there, ready to take me away like they had done so many times before? The fear gnawed at me, but I couldn't let it consume me. I had to focus on getting back to Liam and the kids.

"Do you have family around? Anyone you can call?" the driver asked as he glanced back at me.

"I... I don't know," I stammered, the words catching in my throat. I'm

The driver fell silent for a moment, letting the weight of my words hang in the air. I stared out the window, watching the city pass by in a blur of lights and shadows. Each second felt like an eternity.

When we finally pulled up to my street, my heart dropped. The sight of the police cars parked outside my house sent a wave of dread through me. "No, no, no," I muttered before I flung open the door and raced towards my front door. The taxi driver shouts something about paying him behind me but I ignore it.

An officer stood by the entrance, arms crossed, a look of scrutiny on his face as I approached. "Excuse me, am I allowed in?" I asked, my voice baby above a whisper.

He glanced at me, then nodded curtly. "You can go in."

As I stepped inside, the panic surged anew. The place felt weird as I spotted two officers in the kitchen. One was scribbling notes, while the other, a detective with a sharp gaze, looked up at me with concern.

"Are you alright?" he asked, taking in my disheveled appearance—hospital gown and bare feet.

"I'm... I'm fine," I stammered, though I could hear the tremor in my voice. "I left the hospital. I needed to come home."

The detective exchanged a glance with his colleague before continuing, "We need to ask you a few questions. Are you ready for an interview?"

I nodded, but a wave of panic washed over me. "Where's Liam? Where's my father?"

"Both have been arrested. They're at the local police station," he explained, his tone even but devoid of comfort.

My heart sank. "And the children? What... what about them?"

"Your sister has taken the twins and Ariel," he said. "Jax and Dylan have gone to their dad, as has Harley."

The mention of Dylan being with his father made my stomach turn. "No, no! I can't let that happen. He shouldn't be there!" My voice rose, the fear spilling over.

"I understand this is difficult," the detective said, his eyes softening. "But right now, we need you to focus. We'll do everything we can to ensure the children are safe. We just need to get your account of what happened."

"Fine," I said, my voice shaking but resolute. "Just... just let me see my children, please."

The detective nodded, and I could see the concern etched on his face. "We'll do our best. But first, we need to talk."

I took a deep breath, steeling myself for the questions to come, my mind racing with worry for my children and Liam, of course Liam.

"Alright then," I said, my voice trembling yet firm. "I just need to see my children, please."

The detective nodded, concern evident in his features. "We'll do everything we can to help. But first, we need to have a conversation."

I inhaled deeply, preparing myself for the barrage of questions that awaited me, my thoughts swirling with anxiety for my children and, of course, for Liam.

Just then, my phone rang, jolting me from my thoughts. It was Peter. "Am I allowed to answer this?" I asked the detectives, feeling as though I were in some sort of interrogation room. "It's Harley's dad. He has Harley right now, and I'm really worried it might be important! Harley has autism."

The detective glanced at his colleague before giving me a nod. "Go on, but keep it brief."

I quickly swiped to answer the call, my heart pounding in my chest. "Peter? Is everything alright?"

"Hey, I just wanted to check in. I'm at home with Harley, and I wanted to see how you're doing," he said, his voice steady but laced with concern.

"I'm okay, I think," I replied, glancing at the detectives, who were watching me closely. "But there's been a lot going on. I'm just trying to get back to the kids. Is Harley alright?"

"He's fine, but he's been asking for you," Peter said, his tone softening. "I know things are a bit chaotic right now, but he needs to know you're okay."

"I'm trying my best. Can you keep an eye on him for me?" I pleaded, feeling the weight of my responsibilities pressing down on me. "I don't want him to be scared."

"Of course," Peter reassured me. "Just focus on sorting everything out. I'll keep him entertained until you can come home."

"Thanks, Peter. I really appreciate it," I said, my voice thick with emotion. "I'll get back to you as soon as I can."

At this moment, Peter stood out in my mind as a steady presence, a man transformed since the days when we were together. Once, I had harboured romantic feelings for him, a spark that flickered in the early days of our relationship, but over time, those feelings had faded into a deep, abiding friendship as I explained before. We had navigated the tumultuous waters of co-parenting, and in doing so, had forged a bond that was far more substantial than what we once shared as a couple.

He had a rugged charm about him now, his features more defined, with a slight stubble that added to his appeal. His hair, once perpetually unkempt, was now neatly styled, reflecting the stability he had found in his life. He carried himself with an air of confidence that I hadn't noticed before, a testament to the strides he had made in both his personal and professional life. It was clear that he had worked hard, and the results were evident in the way he presented himself and the pride he took in his role as a father.

What struck me most was the way he had stepped up in his role as a dad. Peter was a fantastic father to Harley, always patient and kind, ensuring that his needs were met with the utmost care. I often saw glimpses of the love he held for Harley in the way he interacted with him, his voice soothing and reassuring. He had become someone who not only provided support but also celebrated the small victories of fatherhood, guiding Harley through challenges with empathy and understanding.

Our dynamic had shifted, but it had matured into something beautiful. I loved him dearly as a friend now, appreciating the support he offered without the complications of romantic entanglements. Our conversations flowed easily, marked by a shared understanding of each other's lives. Liam particularly enjoyed discussing geek culture with Peter, their mutual interests creating a camaraderie that brought a sense of normalcy amidst the chaos some days.

It was heartening to witness how well Peter had done for himself. He had carved out a successful career, and his determination was admirable. He had grown in ways I had once hoped for during our relationship, but now I found joy in his achievements rather than any lingering regret.

As I navigated this challenging moment in my life, I felt grateful for the friendship we had built. It was a solid foundation that allowed us to co-parent effectively, and I knew that regardless of the circumstances, Peter would always be there for Harley—and for me.

The detective's gaze remained steady, his eyes searching mine for a flicker of understanding amidst the turmoil. "First, we need to take a detailed account of what happened leading up to this point. It's crucial for us to understand the context."

I took a deep breath, trying to gather my thoughts. The sterile smell of the kitchen and the hum of the fluorescent lights overhead felt suffocating. "It goes back further than this moment… to my childhood," I began, my voice quivering slightly as memories surged forth.

I hesitated, the weight of what I was about to share heavy on my heart. "My father… he wasn't a good man. He was abusive, and I've carried those scars with me for as long as I can remember. It was a darkness that loomed over my childhood, a fear that never really left. Liam knows about it; I confided in him during the early days of our relationship. He understood the impact it had on me, how it shaped my fears as a parent."

The detective nodded, encouraging me to continue, his expression sympathetic. "And how did this relate to the recent events?"

I swallowed hard, the memories flooding back. "Just a few days ago, my father followed me home after a visit. I thought I was safe, but I felt his presence lurking in the shadows. The day before that, he attempted to hurt me in ways that I thought I had long escaped. I thought I could keep my children safe from him, but the fear of him creeping back into my life was always there, lurking."

The detective's brow furrowed with concern. "And Liam? How did he come to be involved with the knife in the kitchen?"

"Liam was terrified when he found out my father was around. He knew about the abuse, and he felt the weight of the responsibility to protect me and the children. That day, when my father showed up, Liam rushed to the kitchen, grabbing a knife in a moment of panic. He thought he could defend us, that he could confront the threat that had haunted my life for so long."

I took a shuddering breath, feeling the weight of my vulnerability. "It was such a desperate move, but I understood why he did it. He was trying to protect us, to shield me from the past I thought I had escaped. But it escalated everything, and I couldn't let that happen. I couldn't let my children witness that kind of violence."

The detective listened intently, jotting down notes as I spoke. "And what happened after that?"

"Well you must know the rest!" I nervously giggle.

The detective nodded, his expression serious yet compassionate. "You're very brave for sharing this. It's important for us to understand how these past experiences have influenced your current situation."

"I just want to protect my children," I said, my voice thick with emotion. "I don't want them to go through what I did. I'll do whatever it takes to keep them safe."

The detective's eyes softened. "And that's exactly why we're here—to ensure that your children are safe and that you have the support you need. We'll do everything we can to help you navigate this."

The detective's gaze remained steady, his eyes searching mine for a flicker of understanding amidst the turmoil. "First, we need to take a detailed account of what happened leading up to this point. It's crucial for us to understand the context."

I took a deep breath, trying to gather my thoughts. The sterile smell of the kitchen and the hum of the fluorescent lights overhead felt suffocating. "It goes back further than this moment… to my childhood," I began, my voice quivering slightly as memories surged forth.

I hesitated, the weight of what I was about to share heavy on my heart. "My father… he wasn't a good man. He was abusive, and I've carried those scars with me for as long as I can remember. It was a darkness that loomed over my childhood, a fear that never really left. Liam knows about it; I confided in him during the early days of our relationship. He understood the impact it had on me, how it shaped my fears as a parent."

The detective nodded, encouraging me to continue, his expression sympathetic. "And how did this relate to the recent events?"

I swallowed hard, the memories flooding back. "Just a few days ago, my father followed me home after a visit. I thought I was safe, but I felt his presence lurking in the shadows. The day before that, he attempted to hurt me in ways that I thought I had long escaped. I thought I could keep my children safe from him, but the fear of him creeping back into my life was always there, lurking."

The detective's brow furrowed with concern. "And Liam? How did he come to be involved with the knife in the kitchen?"

"Liam was terrified when he found out my father was around. He knew about the abuse, and he felt the weight of the responsibility to protect me and the children. That day, when my father showed up, Liam rushed to the kitchen, grabbing a knife in a moment of panic. He thought he could defend us, that he could confront the threat that had haunted my life for so long."

I took a shuddering breath, feeling the weight of my vulnerability. "It was such a desperate move, but I understood why he did it. He was trying to protect us, to shield me from the past I thought I had escaped. But it escalated everything, and I couldn't let that happen. I couldn't let my children witness that kind of violence."

The detective listened intently, jotting down notes as I spoke. "And what happened after that?"

"The confrontation was intense. I managed to talk Liam down, to convince him that we needed to find a different way to handle it. But the fear was palpable. I felt like my past was clawing its way back into my life, threatening to destroy everything I had fought to build."

The detective nodded, his expression serious yet compassionate. "You're very brave for sharing this. It's important for us to understand how these past experiences have influenced your current situation."

"I just want to protect my children," I said, my voice thick with emotion. "I don't want them to go through what I did. I'll do whatever it takes to keep them safe."

The detective's eyes softened. "And that's exactly why we're here—to ensure that your children are safe and that you have the support you need. We'll do everything we can to help you navigate this."

As I took in his words, a wave of hopelessness crashed over me. The reality of my situation settled in once more. Losing baby Scarlett. The thought of my other children being taken away left a gaping hole in my heart, and now Liam was arrested, caught in the crossfire of a situation that spiralled more and more beyond our control. My father, the very source of my torment, would likely evade any serious consequences, once again slipping through the cracks of the system that had failed me so many times before.

"Is this really how it ends?" I whispered, more to myself than to the detective. "Am I really losing everything?"

The detective's expression softened, but I could see the limits of what he could do. I needed more than just assurances; I needed backup, someone who understood the gravity of my past and could stand with me in this fight. My thoughts turned to my sister, Lucy. She had witnessed the abuse, shared in the trauma of our childhood, and might just be the voice I needed to validate my fears and experiences. Yeah we might hate each other at times, but we are grown up now and our kids come first.

"I need to call Lucy," I said suddenly, my resolve hardening. "She has to know what's happening. She can help."

The detective nodded, offering me a small measure of support. "That sounds like a good idea. Make the call."

I fumbled for my phone once again, my fingers trembling as I scrolled through my contacts. Lucy's name glowed on the screen, and I hesitated, the weight of what I was about to ask pressing heavily on me. But I knew I needed her.

"Come on, pick up," I muttered under my breath as I pressed the call button. After a few rings, her familiar voice came through, filled with concern. "Hello?"

"Lucy, it's me," I said, trying to keep my voice steady. "I need your help."

"What's going on?" she asked, her tone shifting to one of urgency. "You sound upset."

"It's… it's about Dad," I stammered, emotions threatening to overwhelm me. "He followed me home, and things got really bad. Liam tried to protect me and the kids, and now he's in trouble. I'm scared, Lucy. I don't know what to do. They're taking the children away from me, and I can't let that happen."

There was a pause on the other end, and I could hear her sharp intake of breath. "Oh my God, are you alright? What happened?"

"I'm okay, but I feel so hopeless," I admitted, tears brimming in my eyes. "I lost Scarlett, and now my other children are at risk. I need you to back me up. You know what he did to us. You saw it all."

"I remember everything," she said, her voice resolute. "I'm so sorry you're going through this. I'll stand by you. Just tell me what you need."

"Can you come to mine? I need someone who can testify to what we endured. I need them to understand that I'm not the enemy here. My father is the real threat," I urged, desperation creeping into my voice.

"Of course, I'll be there," Lucy replied without hesitation. "I'll make sure they know the truth. We can't let him win again."

A rush of relief flooded through me at her words. "Thank you, Lucy. I don't know what I would do without you."

"Just hang in there. I'll be there soon," she reassured me, and as we hung up, a flicker of hope ignited within .me. Perhaps I wasn't completely lost after all

I paced the living room, anxiety coiling in my stomach as the minutes dragged on. I glanced at the clock, willing it to move faster. The atmosphere felt heavy with anticipation, and I offered a weak smile to the few officers present as I fidgeted. "Would anyone like some tea or coffee? Or perhaps a biscuit?" I asked, my voice tinged with nervous energy. It felt like a futile attempt to distract myself from the overwhelming dread that hung over me.

As I waited, I could feel the weight of my past pressing down on me, suffocating and relentless. I thought of Lucy, my little sister, and the bond we had forged through shared trauma. I hoped she would arrive soon, bringing with her the comfort of familiarity and understanding.

Finally, the door swung open, and there she was—Lucy, with her familiar tousled hair and wide eyes filled with concern. Without a moment's hesitation, she rushed towards me, enveloping me in a tight hug. The warmth of her embrace felt like a lifeline, and I couldn't hold back the tears that spilled down my cheeks.

"Oh, Lucy," I sobbed, the weight of everything crashing down around us. "I'm so glad you're here."

As much as we had fought and bickered over the years, as much as I sometimes hated her for the things she had done, I loved her dearly. We had both been victims of our father's cruelty, and in that moment, I felt a deep connection to her pain.

"I'm here, I'm here," she whispered, holding me tightly as we both cried, our shoulders shaking with the release of pent-up emotions. "We're going to get through this together."

After a few moments, we pulled back, our faces streaked with tears. "Are you ready for this, sis?" I asked, my voice trembling.

Lucy nodded, determination shining in her eyes. "I'm ready. Let's do this."

We settled into the living room, a space that had seen countless memories, both good and bad. I began to recount the years of abuse we had endured at the hands of our father. "He didn't just hurt me," I said, my voice growing steadier. "He hurt Mum too. She was disabled, and he took advantage of that. Nobody believed us. We were trapped in that house of horrors, and the system failed us time and again."

Lucy listened intently, her face a mixture of anguish and resolve as I recounted the memories that had haunted me for so long. "I remember when I was just seven years old, covered in chicken pox. I was so uncomfortable, so miserable. Instead of caring for me, he slapped me across the face, blaming me for being sick. I felt so small and helpless, like I was somehow at fault for my own suffering."

I paused, the memory flooding back with vivid clarity. "He wouldn't even let me eat, refusing to give me food until I stopped crying. I was terrified, hungry, and in pain, and all I wanted was a little kindness. But he twisted everything, made me feel like I deserved it. It was like living in a nightmare."

Lucy's expression was painful to see as she nodded in understanding. "I remember those days too. It was like he thrived on our fear, and we were powerless to stop him."

I took a shaky breath, feeling the urge to spill everything out. "And losing baby Scarlett… it's like a knife in my heart. I can't shake the guilt that maybe if I had been stronger, if I had done something differently, she'd still be here. I went through so many tumultuous relationships, trying to find someone who could love me and my children. But it all fell apart."

As I spoke, I began to ramble, the words flowing out of me like a torrent. "And Dad with the prostitutes! I can't believe I lived with that man for so long. I remember finding things in his room, things he tried to hide. He thought he could keep everything a secret, but we knew. And then there was the time… the near childhood pregnancy. I thought I was going to be stuck in that cycle forever, just like Mum. It felt like I was suffocating."

I paused, feeling a wave of emotions crash over me. "I remember how he would come home from his cash in hand jobs, always angry. It was like he was a monster in our home, and we were just waiting for the next attack. The way he would lash out, the yelling, the threats—I thought I wouldn't survive it."

Lucy reached for my hand, squeezing it tightly as I continued to pour out my heart. "There were times I tried to tell someone, a teacher, a friend, but I was always met with disbelief. How could anyone imagine that a father could be so cruel? I felt invisible, like my pain didn't matter. The system was supposed to protect us, but it failed every time. They never saw the bruises on our souls."

I glanced at the officers nearby, who were listening intently. "I know I can be scattered sometimes, especially with my ADHD," I admitted, feeling the need to explain my ramblings. "But it's just so overwhelming to think about everything. The chaos in my head, the memories, all of it pouring out at once."

One of the officers, a kind-looking woman, approached us gently. "Take your time," she said softly. "We're here to listen and support

I took a deep breath and shifted the weight of my emotions as I glanced at Lucy, my heart aching for everything that had transpired. "How is Liam?" I asked, my voice trembling slightly. "I can't stop thinking about him. He's innocent in all of this, Lucy. He was just trying to protect us, to keep the children safe. I want him home."

Lucy's expression softened, and she nodded. "I know, I've been thinking about him too. He didn't deserve to get caught up in this mess. He loves you and your kids, and he just acted out of fear. It's heartbreaking to think of him there, worried and alone."

"Exactly!" I exclaimed, feeling a mix of frustration and sadness. "He was just trying to do what any decent person would do. I can't believe they took him away like he's the villain. It's all so twisted. My father is the real monster here, and yet Liam is the one who's paying the price for trying to defend us."

Lucy took a moment to gather her thoughts. "I know it's hard, but we have to focus on getting him out. We need to show everyone the truth—that Liam was only trying to protect you and the kids. We can't let this go on any longer."

"Thank you, Lucy," I say. 'I just want to get through this. I want us all to be safe and together again. I can't bear the thought of Liam being treated like a criminal when he was just trying to protect us from the real threat."

"Then we'll do everything we can to make that happen," Lucy affirmed, her voice strong and steady. "Let's start gathering everything we need, and we'll make sure Liam is back where he belongs—home with you and the kids!"

I turn to Lucy, who was shaking her head with a smirk. "Seriously, though, why are you in a hospital gown and shoeless? You look like you've just escaped from a really bad soap opera."

I let out a bitter laugh, wiping my eyes. "Welcome to my life! I came here in a panic, and somehow ended up in this ridiculous getup. I mean, really? What's next, a dramatic monologue about my tragic existence?"

Lucy snorted, trying to suppress her laughter. "I can see it now: 'As the World Turns: The Hospital Gown Chronicles!'"

We both chuckled, but the laughter felt hollow, echoing in the dark corners of our reality. The officers had handed me a stack of leaflets on historic child abuse, domestic abuse, and counselling programs, which I had taken out of courtesy. "Thanks for that," I said sarcastically, rolling my eyes as I tossed them into the nearest bin. "Like I'm going to sit down with a cup of tea and read about how screwed up my life is. Brilliant idea!"

The police drive away in the distance.

Lucy shook her head, a grin still on her face but her eyes reflecting the seriousness of our situation. "You've really outdone yourself this time."

I took a deep breath, trying to shift the conversation back to something meaningful. "So, how are Ariel and the twins doing? I hope they're managing okay."

Lucy's expression softened, and she nodded. "I left them with Nan. They're fine. She has the baby monitors in use, so she can keep an eye on them at all times. I made sure the schools are informed about everything going on, and I told them not to let anyone else pick Ariel up'

Relief washed over me, but it was tinged with a sense of urgency. "Thank God for Nan. I don't know what I would do without her. I just wish I could be there with them right now."

"They miss you, but Nan won't leave their side," Lucy reassured me. "She's making sure they feel safe and loved, even in all this. They're holding up surprisingly well, considering everything."

I sighed, the weight of everything crashing in on me again. "In all this madness, I feel like I've forgotten everything. I just want life to go back to normal. Or else, I'll end up in the grave with Scarlett, and what kind of ending is that? 'And she lived unhappily ever after!'"

Lucy's eyes filled with empathy as she listened. "I get it. You want to protect them from all of this, to shield them from the darkness that has haunted us for so long. But you're doing everything you can right now. You're fighting for Liam, for your kids, for a future that's bright'

"I just can't shake this feeling of helplessness," I admitted, my voice thick with emotion. "Every time I close my eyes, I see Scarlett's face. I feel like I'm drowning in grief. It's like I'm standing at the edge of a cliff, and I'm terrified of falling into that darkness. I want to be strong for Ariel and the twins and the boys but I don't know how."

Lucy leaned closer, her hand resting on mine. "You don't have to have all the answers right now. Just take it one day at a time. We'll figure this out together. You're not alone in this fight. I promise."

I nodded, grateful for her support, but the weight of it all still felt heavy on my heart. "I just want to wake up one day and find that everything is okay again. I want to breathe without feeling this constant pressure in my chest. But here I am, in a hospital gown, shoeless, and contemplating my next move like it's a game of chess in an empty pub."

"Well, if you're going to do that, at least make sure to order a pint while you're at it," Lucy replied sarcastically, trying to lighten the mood again.

As we sat in that living room, surrounded by the echoes of our shared trauma, I felt an overwhelming sense of urgency rising within me. I wouldn't let the darkness swallow me whole.

Six months later

The days blurred into each other as we prepared for the court case against my father. The air once again suffocating and relentless. I could hardly think straight, my mind racing with thoughts of what I would have to face. The moment the court date was set, dread settled in my stomach, turning my insides into knots.

The courtroom itself felt like a cold, room, devoid of comfort. I remember standing there, my heart pounding in my chest as I looked around at the faces—some sympathetic, others judgmental. I felt exposed, like a fish out of water, struggling to breathe. My father sat on the other side, a picture of defiance, as if he believed he was untouchable.

When it was my turn to testify, I felt like I was walking into a lion's den. I took a deep breath and stepped forward, the weight of the truth pressing down on me. The judge looked at me expectantly, and I could feel the eyes of the courtroom boring into my soul.

"I was a few years old when I first realised something was wrong," I began, my voice shaking but gaining strength as I recounted the horrors of my childhood. "One time I was covered in chicken pox, and instead of caring for me, he slapped me across the face, blaming me for being sick. He wouldn't let me eat until I stopped crying. I felt so small, so worthless."

With each word, I felt the walls of the courtroom close in on me, and I fought to keep my composure. "He brought home prostitutes, thinking it was normal, he had sex with them when I was in the car. He would come home angry, and lash out at us. We were terrified. We wanted to escape but there was nowhere to go. I felt trapped. He let people fuck me, touch me, he fucked me himself, one time he nearly got me pregnant!"

The prosecutor nodded, encouraging me to continue. "I remember nights spent hiding in my room, listening to the screams and the chaos. I remember the fear, the desperation. I never thought I would see the day he would be held accountable for his actions."

As I spoke, I could see my father's face twisting in anger and disbelief. It was as if my words were a physical blow to him, and I felt a strange mix of fear and exhilaration. I was finally telling the truth, and no one could silence me now.

But as the testimony dragged on, I could feel the weight of my family's judgment pressing down on me. They had always been the silent witnesses to our suffering, but now, as I stood there in the spotlight, I could sense their disapproval. They were ashamed of me for speaking out, for dragging our dirty laundry into the light.

By the time I finished, I was exhausted, both physically and emotionally. The relief was short-lived, though. As I stepped down from the stand, I caught a glimpse of my family's faces—they were twisted with anger, disappointment, and betrayal. They had disowned me for confronting our past, for daring to expose the monster that had terrorised us for so long.

The verdict came down swiftly. My father was arrested on charges of abuse, and the relief was bittersweet. The courtroom erupted in a mix of gasps and whispers, and I couldn't help but feel a sense of triumph. But it was short-lived, as the reality of my family's rejection sank in. They turned their backs on me, refusing to see the truth I had fought so hard to reveal.

In the aftermath, I stepped away from my job, unable to return to a life that felt so fractured. The corporate world seemed trivial in comparison to the chaos I had just endured. I had spent years trying to climb the ladder, only to realise that the foundation had been built on lies and secrets.

Meanwhile, Liam was released on self-defense charges, but the relief of his freedom came with its own complications. I had to confront the truth that had been lurking in the shadows—just before the knife incident, I had found out about his infidelity. I had been blindsided, the betrayal cutting deeper than any knife ever could.

The night I discovered his cheating, I felt like the ground had been ripped from beneath me. I had come home early, hoping to surprise him, only to find him in a compromising position with someone else. The rage and heartbreak coursed through me like a poison, and I couldn't breathe.

When I confronted him, the fight that ensued was explosive. I had never seen him so defensive, so desperate to explain himself. "It didn't mean anything!" he had shouted, his voice rising in panic. "I was confused! I didn't think it would get this far!"

"Confused?" I had spat back, feeling the tears burning in my eyes. "You think that gives you an excuse? You were supposed to be my partner, Liam! And now you've ruined everything!"

After that night, everything changed. Even as we tried to piece together what had happened, the fractures in our relationship deepened. I wanted to be there for him, to support him through the aftermath of the court case, but the betrayal loomed large, a dark cloud hanging over us.

We drifted apart, the weight of our shared trauma pulling us in opposite directions. I found myself drowning in a sea of anger and sadness, while he struggled to cope with the consequences of his actions and the fallout from the court case, losing Scarlett, the hassle of the growing twins, the traumas.

Eventually, we both knew it was over. The love that once connected us was frayed and battered, a mere shadow of what it had been. I had lost my family, and now, I was losing Liam too.

As I sat alone in the living room, the silence deafening, I realised who I was left with nothing but the remnants of a life that had once held promise. I thought of the future I had envisioned, a future that now felt like a cruel joke played by fate.

I had fought tooth and nail for my freedom, for the truth, and yet here I was, staring into the abyss of my own despair. I had lost everything, and the darkness threatened to swallow me whole.

The weeks dragged on in a blur of meetings and discussions with social services, each appointment feeling like an uphill battle. I found myself sitting in sterile offices, surrounded by professionals who seemed more interested in ticking boxes than understanding the chaos of my life. Each meeting brought up the same questions, the same doubts, and I was left feeling like I was under a microscope, my every action scrutinized.

But I was determined to get my children back. I endured the long hours in those offices, pouring my heart out about the love I had for them and the lengths I would go to ensure their safety and happiness. I met with social workers, family support teams, and even had to sit down with the fathers of my children. It was an odd mix of emotions—some supportive, others simply there to fulfil their obligations.

Surprisingly, Xavier complied with the process. He seemed to understand how important it was for the children to have a stable environment, even if it meant working with me. His demeanour was professional, and I found myself respecting him more than I ever had, even if he was still a complicated presence in my life. We exchanged updates and made arrangements regarding the children's needs, and I could see that he genuinely wanted what was best for them.

With every meeting, I felt a flicker of hope, but it was tempered by frustration. The social services were cautious, wanting to ensure that I had a solid plan in place. I spent hours discussing strategies, organising schedules, and outlining how I intended to provide for my children. I was adamant about demonstrating my commitment to making things work.

It was during these meetings that I found myself getting closer to Peter. We often ended up in the same waiting room, exchanging nervous glances and awkward small talk. As we shared our concerns and hopes for all the children but especially Harley. , I discovered a very supportive ally. He seemed genuinely interested in ensuring that his son had a stable and loving environment, and our conversations began to shift from formality to camaraderie.

Meanwhile, Dylan finally began to attend counselling sessions. I had pushed him to open up, hoping that talking to someone would ease the anxiety that seemed to be growing like a shadow over him. He was reluctant at first, his defences built high, but I promised him that it was a safe space. However, the change was slow. Each session felt like a monumental task, and while he was willing to go, it was evident that the progress was minimal. His anxiety shone through every day, exacerbated by the presence of PDA at school and the pressures of being a child in a turbulent environment.

"Why can't people just leave me alone?" he would mutter, his frustration palpable. I could see it wearing on him, the weight of expectation and the fear of judgment gnawing at his spirit. I wished I could take it all away, but all I could do was support him and remind him that he wasn't alone.

Jax, on the other hand, presented a different challenge. When it came time for him to return home from his father's, he was adamantly against it. The manipulation and gaslighting from his father had taken a toll. I could see the conflict in his eyes, the way he hesitated to make eye contact. "He says it's your fault for everything that's happened," he confessed one night, his voice barely above a whisper. "He says if you had just behaved and been a good mum, things would be fine."

I felt a surge of anger at the thought of me being made responsible for this. "I didn't do anything wrong, Jax. It's not my fault," I assured him, kneeling down to meet his gaze. "You deserve to feel safe and loved, not to be involved in someone else's mistakes."

But the doubt lingered in his eyes, and I knew it would take time to untangle the mess his father had created in his mind. I tried to reassure him, to let him know that our home was a safe place, but the scars of his father's words were deep.

Weeks turned into what felt like an eternity, but finally, the day came when social services deemed it safe for me to have the children back. The relief was overwhelming, but it was also mixed with trepidation. I wanted to be the mother they needed, but would they be able to adjust after everything that had happened?

When I finally walked into the house with Dylan, Jax, and my son, it felt surreal. The walls were the same, the furniture unchanged, but everything felt different. I could feel the weight of their gazes, the uncertainty in the air.

"Home sweet home," I said, attempting to lighten the mood, but the tension lingered. Dylan plopped down on the couch, his head buried in his hands, while Jax stood stiffly by the doorway, looking as if he might bolt at any moment.

"Are you sure it's okay to be here?" Jax asked, his voice trembling. I could see the worry etched on his face, and it broke my heart.

"Absolutely," I replied, walking over to him and placing a reassuring hand on his shoulder. "This is where we belong, together. No one can take that away from us."

I tried to create a sense of normalcy, but it was clear that our return would be a process. The children were still grappling with the aftermath of everything they had faced, and I knew it wouldn't be easy.

As the weeks turned into months, I found a sense of rhythm settling back into our lives, albeit a rhythm touched by the remnants of our past. The twins had eased somewhat, but their difficulties completely disappeared. My mind was still haunted by the fear that they might die in their sleep, a shadow that loomed over every night. I had worked tirelessly to create a safe environment for them, filled with routines and reassurances that helped them manage their anxieties. Every time they drifted off, I found myself checking on them repeatedly even still now, my heart racing with each quiet moment.

One of our cherished routines was visiting Scarlett's grave. Every few weeks, I would gather the children—my heart swelling with both pride and sorrow as they leaned into this shared experience. We would bring fresh sunflowers and little trinkets—mostly elephants, their shared favourite since they were small. They represented strength, memory, and love to us, and I would watch as they carefully placed their offerings on her grave, whispering their thoughts and hopes to their sister. It was a bittersweet moment, one that brought us together while reminding us of the fragility of life.

Now, in the exact present day, I found myself nestled in the warmth of the bath, the water soothing my weary bones. The twins were asleep in their crib, their soft breaths a comforting sound amidst the silence of the house. Jax was in the living room, lost in a video game, while Ariel snuggled on her mid-sleeper, engrossed in her tablet. Harley was with Peter, expected back for dinner later, which left me with a rare moment of peace. I assumed Dylan was also off somewhere, probably absorbed in his PlayStation, blissfully unaware of the mania that sometimes lurked within our family.

As I relaxed, the warmth enveloping me like a cocoon, I let my mind drift. I thought about how far we had come, the battles we had fought, and the love that bound us together. But just as I started to sink deeper into that comforting reverie, the tranquility shattered.

The bathroom door creaked open. I turned my head, startled, as now Ten-year-old Dylan stepped in. My heart raced, not because of the intrusion, but because he was holding a knife. A sparkle of metal caught the light caught the bathroom loght, piercing through the warmth of my bubble bath like a cold spike of fear.

"Mum!" he exclaimed, his eyes wide with a manic excitement that sent chills down my spine. "Look! I know how fun knives are now!"

"Dylan, put that down!" My voice was sharp, urgency lacing my words as I instinctively tried to cover myself, feeling so exposed and vulnerable. But he didn't seem to hear me. Instead, he grinned, his laughter bubbling up as he paced around the bathroom, waving the knife in the air like it was a toy.

"Liam looked so powerful with a knife! I want to be powerful too!" His laughter echoed, bouncing off the tiled walls, a sound that felt hollow and unsettling. I couldn't shake the feeling that his expression mirrored my father's in those dark moments, the joy twisted into something sinister.

"Dylan, please, just put the knife down," I urged, my heart racing. I felt trapped, the bathwater suddenly too warm, too confining. I was completely at his mercy, laid bare in every sense, and fear clutched at my throat.

But he just kept hopping around the room, his laughter growing more manic with each leap. "Mum, look at me! I'm powerful! I can do anything!" He twirled the knife, the blade glinting dangerously close to my face, and I felt my breath catch in my throat.

"Dylan, stop!" I shouted, my voice cracking as panic set in. "You're scaring me!"

His eyes sparkled with a wildness I had never seen before, and for a moment, I could only see a reflection of my father in him once again—an echo of that same chaotic energy. I felt a wave of nausea rise within me, the memories of my childhood flooding back like a broken dam.

Suddenly, the room spun, and I was no longer just a mother in a bath. I was a young girl again, trying to hide from the monster that lived in my house, the one who wielded power with fear and violence. "Put it down, Dylan!" I pleaded, my voice barely above a whisper now.

But he just laughed, that manic sound filling the air, and before I could react, he lunged forward, the knife a blur of silver in his small hand. I barely had time to register what was happening when I felt a sharp pain in my chest, a sensation that took my breath away.

The world slowed as I looked down, disbelief washing over me. The knife was buried deep in my flesh, blood staining the water around me, a dark, swirling reminder of what had just transpired. Dylan's laughter echoed, unsettling and haunting, as if it was all a twisted game to him.

"Look, Mum! I'm so powerful!" he shouted, joy radiating from him as if he had just accomplished a great feat. My heart raced, panic clawing at my insides as I gasped for air, the warmth of the bath fading into an abyss as the reality of the moment sank in.

Surely this wasn't real. I blinked, trying to process the horror unfolding before me. The laughter continued, insistent and jarring, and I felt the darkness creeping in at the edges of my vision.

"Dylan," I tried to speak, but my voice was a mere whisper now, the weight of the world crashing down on me. "Please… help me…"

But my words were swallowed by his laughter, a sound that echoed in my ears, mixing with the rushing of blood in my veins. I felt myself slipping away, the warmth of the bath fading into an abyss as the reality of the moment sank in.

And just like that, I was left staring into the void, the darkness closing in, with my son's face—the one I had fought so hard to protect—looming over me like a spectre.

I jolted awake, the remnants of the nightmare clinging to me like a shroud of darkness. The familiar surroundings of my bathroom flooded my senses, the gentle sound of water lapping against the sides of the tub grounding me. I was alive; the knife was not buried in my chest, and Dylan was not holding it in a manic frenzy. But the relief was fleeting, replaced by an unsettling sense of dread that lingered in my mind.

I sat up in the bath, the water cool against my skin, and took deep, shaky breaths, willing my heart to slow. The vividness of the dream echoed in my thoughts—the laughter, the fear, the feeling of vulnerability. I looked around, half-expecting to see Dylan's mischievous face peeking around the corner, but the house was silent.

As I climbed out of the bath, the reality of the evening settled over me. I wrapped a towel around myself and stepped into the hallway, hearing the faint sound of video game gunfire from Jax's room. I made my way to the living room, where Jax was still engrossed in his game, and Ariel was happily snuggled on her mid-sleeper, absorbed in her tablet.

"Hey, you two," I called out, forcing a smile as I tried to shake off the lingering shadows of my dream. "Dinner's going to be ready soon. Harley's with Peter; they'll be here in a bit."

"Okay, Mum!" Jax shouted back, his focus unwavering as he raced his character across the screen. Ariel looked up, her eyes sparkling. "Can I help with dinner?" she asked, her enthusiasm a bright spot in my otherwise frazzled mind.

"Of course, love. We can make it a family affair." I felt the warmth of her excitement cut through the remnants of my nightmare, and for a moment, I thought maybe we could find solace in the mundane joys of life.

But as I began to prepare dinner, the unease from the dream crept back in. What if it was a warning? I tried to shake off the thought, reminding myself that nightmares were just that—nightmares. Yet, the fear of losing my children nagged at me, a constant reminder of the fragility of life.

The evening passed, and the smell of pasta filled the kitchen as the children and I set the table. When Harley and Peter arrived, they brought laughter and joy, a welcomed distraction that pushed the remnants of the nightmare to the back of my mind. We sat around the table, sharing stories and jokes, the kind of normalcy I clung to fiercely.

But as the night wore on, the feeling of dread returned, gnawing at the edges of my thoughts. I kept glancing toward Dylan's empty chair, a hollow reminder of the chaos that sometimes lurked beneath our surface.

After dinner, the children scattered to pursue their activities, and I found myself cleaning up alone. The laughter faded into the background, replaced by an unsettling silence that hung in the air. I felt a chill run down my spine as I recalled the dream—the laughter, the knife, the power.

Just as I finished washing the dishes, I heard a noise from the hallway, a soft but distinct sound. My heart raced as I turned to see Dylan standing there, his eyes wide, a strange smile on his face. "Mum, can I show you something?" he asked, his voice eerily calm.

"Sure, sweetheart. What is it?" I replied, trying to keep my tone light despite the unease creeping back into my chest.

He beckoned me toward his room, and I followed, my instincts screaming at me. As we entered, I noticed the room was dimly lit, shadows creeping into the corners. My blood ran cold as I spotted something glinting on his desk.

"Dylan, what have you got there?" I asked, my voice trembling as I stepped closer.

He turned to me, a gleeful expression on his face, and held out his hand. In it, he clutched a small, shiny knife—one I recognised from the drawer in the kitchen.

"I found this! Isn't it cool?" he exclaimed, his voice dripping with excitement. "I can be powerful just like Liam!"

"Dylan, put that down right now," I said, my heart pounding in my chest. My mind raced, the dream flooding back with terrifying clarity. "You shouldn't have that!"

But he just giggled, that manic laughter echoing in my ears, and I felt the walls closing in, the memory of the dream replaying in my mind like a broken record.

"Dylan, please! You're scaring me!" I shouted, stepping back as he waved the knife around, the blade glinting dangerously close to my face. The child I loved seemed to have vanished, replaced by a version of him that felt foreign and terrifying. I could see shadows of my past flickering in his eyes, and it made my skin crawl.

He just kept hopping around the room, laughter spilling from his lips, filled with a manic energy that made my heart race. "Mum, look at me! I'm powerful! I can do anything!" He twirled the knife, the blade glinting in the dim light, and I felt my breath catch in my throat.

"Dylan, stop!" I shouted, my voice cracking as panic set in. "You're scaring me!"

His eyes sparkled with a wildness I had never seen before, and for a moment, I could only see a reflection of my father in him—an echo of that same chaotic energy. I felt a wave of nausea rise within me, the memories of my childhood flooding back like a broken dam, and I knew I had to act quickly.

"Dylan, please!" I begged, my voice rising in desperation as I lunged forward to grab the knife. But he dodged away, a gleeful look on his face.

"Catch me if you can, Mum!" he shouted, darting around the room, and I felt the world spinning out of control. My instincts kicked in, but fear paralysed me.

"Dylan, put it down!" I screamed, my heart racing as I lunged once more. But he was too quick, and in a flash, he darted toward me, waving the knife as if it were a toy.

"Mum, look how powerful I am!" he shouted, and before I could react, he lunged forward. The world slowed as I saw the knife coming toward me, and I felt a sharp pain in my chest—a sickening reminder of the nightmare I had thought I'd escaped.

As I stumbled back, clutching my chest, the room spun around me. Blood began to seep through my fingers, staining my clothes, as I struggled to process what was happening. The pain was overwhelming, and the warmth of life began to ebb away. Dylan's laughter echoed, unsettling and haunting, as if it was all a twisted game to him.

"Look, Mum! I'm so powerful!" he shouted, joy radiating from him as if he had just accomplished a great feat. My heart raced, panic clawing at my insides as I gasped for air, the warmth of the room fading into an abyss as the reality of the moment sank in.

Surely this wasn't real. I blinked, trying to process the horror unfolding before me. The laughter continued, insistent and jarring, and I felt the darkness creeping in at the edges of my vision.

"Dylan," I tried to speak, but my voice was a mere whisper now, the weight of the world crashing down on me. "Please… help me…"

But my words were swallowed by his laughter, a sound that echoed in my ears, mixing with the rushing of blood in my veins. I felt myself slipping away, the warmth of the bath fading into an abyss as the reality of the moment sank in.

And as my vision faded, Dylan's laughter ringing in my ears, I understood that the battle was lost—forever trapped in a nightmare I could never awaken from.

Continuation:

I awoke to the incessant beeping of machines, the sound jarring and foreign. The harsh fluorescent lights overhead pierced through my eyelids, forcing me to squint against their brightness. Panic surged within me as I instinctively attempted to move, only to find myself restrained. Confusion settled in as I tried to piece together the fragments of my memory.

"Catch me if you can, Mum!" echoed in my mind, followed by the haunting laughter of Dylan, the last sound I remembered before everything went dark. I blinked, desperately searching my surroundings—a hospital room, cold and uninviting. The smell of antiseptic hung heavily in the air, and the beeping of the heart monitor seemed to grow louder, syncing with my racing heart.

As I looked down, I noticed the bandages wrapped around my chest, the pressure of them a constant reminder of the pain I'd endured. I shifted slightly, and a sharp jolt of agony shot through me, sending waves of discomfort radiating from the centre of my body. I instinctively glanced down to find the bandages stained with crimson, a stark contrast against the white fabric. The memories flooded back—the knife, the laughter, the moment of impact.

I had suffered a severe stab wound, a jagged gash that had sliced through muscle and flesh. The doctors had stitched me up, but the stitches, though neat, were a grim reminder of the chaos that had led me here. I could almost feel the sharpness of the blade, the way it had cut through skin and sinew, leaving behind a raw vulnerability that echoed my emotional state.

"Dylan!" I gasped, the name escaping my lips like a prayer. "Where is he?"

A nurse rushed in at the sound of my voice, her expression shifting from routine professionalism to concern. "Bea! You're awake!" she exclaimed, moving swiftly to my side. "You've been unconscious for several hours. You sustained a severe stab wound, but you're stable now."

"Dylan!" I cried, my voice cracking with desperation. "Where is my son? Is he okay?"

GThe nurse hesitated, glancing back toward the door as if gauging the situation. "He's being cared for. He's safe, I promise," she said gently. "But you need to take it easy. You're still recovering."

My heart sank at the nurse's words. What had happened? How had things spiraled so far out of control? "Did… did I hurt him?" I asked, dread pooling in my stomach.

"No, Bea. You need to focus on healing," the nurse replied, her voice soothing. "You were injured during the incident, but Dylan is being looked after by family and professionals who understand his needs."

The weight of those words pressed down on me, and I felt a mix of relief and guilt. The last thing I remembered was Dylan with the knife, his laughter echoing like a dark omen in my mind. Had I really been so helpless to protect him?

As the nurse continued to check my vitals, my thoughts spiralled. Memories of my father, the chaos, the violence—everything seemed to swirl around me like a tempest. I had fought so hard to escape that darkness, to protect my children from the shadows of my past. But here I was, a victim of my own fears, trapped in a cycle that felt unbreakable.

Hours passed before the nurse returned, and when she did, she was accompanied by a familiar face—Lucy. My heart soared at the sight of my sister, but it quickly turned to dread as I noted the worry etched on her features. "Bea! Thank God you're awake!" she exclaimed, rushing to my side.

"Lucy, what happened? Where's Dylan?" My voice trembled, fear flooding my senses as I searched her eyes for answers.

"Dylan is with Nan," Lucy replied, her voice steady but laced with concern. "He's safe, but he's been through a lot. He's been acting out since the incident."

I felt my heart drop. "What do you mean? What happened?"

Lucy took a deep breath, her expression serious. "After everything, he panicked. The police were called, and they took him to the hospital for evaluation. They wanted to ensure he was okay after the chaos that ensued."

I felt the weight of guilt crash over me like a wave. "I can't believe this is happening. I never meant to scare him. I just wanted to protect him!"

"I know, Bea. But he needs you now more than ever. He needs to know he's loved, even when things get difficult," Lucy said, her voice filled with empathy. "You both do."

The reality of those words pressed down on me, and I felt a wave of sadness wash over me. I had known Dylan struggled, but to hear him voice his fears so openly was both heartbreaking and enlightening. "I know that I can't carry this burden alone. I need to do better for him and for myself," I said, my voice quivering with emotion.

As the nurse re-entered the room, her expression softening, she said, "Bea, I'm glad you're awake. We need to discuss the next steps for your recovery and Dylan's treatment."

I nodded, my mind racing with thoughts of my son. "I want to see him," I insisted. "I need to talk to him."

The nurse exchanged a glance with Lucy before nodding. "Alright, we can arrange that, but you need to take it easy. You've been through a lot."

As the nurse prepared to escort me to the pediatric ward, I felt a rush of anxiety. I had fought so hard to protect my children, but now I felt like I was losing control of everything. The darkness threatened to swallow me whole, but I pushed it aside, focusing instead on the love I had for Dylan.

When we arrived at the pediatric ward, my heart raced. I spotted Dylan sitting on a hospital bed, his small frame curled up in a ball, a frown etched on his face as he stared down at the floor. The sight tore at my heart. "Dylan!" I called, rushing to his side.

He looked up, his eyes wide with surprise and confusion. "Mum…" he whispered, his voice barely audible.

I knelt beside him, wrapping my arms around him in a tight embrace. "I'm so sorry, sweetheart. I never wanted to scare you."

He hesitated for a moment before relaxing into my embrace, his small body trembling against mine. "I was just trying to be powerful," he said, his voice muffled against my shoulder. "I didn't mean for any of this to happen."

"I know, love. I know," I soothed, holding him tighter as tears began to flow. "We'll figure this out together. You're not alone in this."

As we sat there, wrapped in each other's arms, I felt a flicker of hope ignite within me. The darkness might still linger, but in this moment, we were together, and that was enough to carry us through the storm.

In the days that followed, Dylan and I began our journey toward healing together. With the support of therapists and a newfound determination, we navigated the complexities of our emotions, learning to express ourselves in healthier ways. Each session was a step forward, a chance to confront the pain that had shaped our lives.

I also reached out to family and friends, seeking a support network that could help us through this difficult time. Lucy became a constant presence, offering her strength and understanding as we both grappled with the aftermath of our father's actions. Together, we shared our stories, bonded over our experiences, and created a safe space for open communication.

As time went on, I found ways to channel my pain into advocacy. I began volunteering at local organisations that supported survivors of abuse, using my voice to raise awareness and help others who had faced similar struggles. The act of giving back became a source of empowerment, reminding me that I was not defined by my past but rather by my resilience.

Dylan, too, found solace in creative outlets. He discovered a love for art, expressing his emotions through drawings and paintings that conveyed the depth of his experiences. As he poured his heart onto the canvas, he began to heal, transforming his pain into something beautiful and powerful.

Months passed, and the weight of the past began to lift. I stood at Scarlett's grave once again alone this time , a bouquet of vibrant sunflowers in hand, feeling the warmth of the sun on my skin. The memories of loss and pain would always linger, but I had learned to embrace the love that remained.

"I promise to keep moving forward," I whispered, tears streaming down my cheeks. "You will always be a part of us, and I will make sure your siblings know the love you brought into our lives."

As I rose, I felt a sense of peace wash over me, a newfound strength within me. I turned to head home, ready to embrace the future with my children by my side, we will get through this.

Chapter 7: Unexpected Reunions

As I stood in the kitchen, the familiar scents of bubbling tomato sauce and melting cheese filling the air, I couldn't help but feel a sense of contentment wash over me. The laughter and chatter of my children echoed from the living room, a symphony of joy that I had once feared I might never hear again.

In the months since the incident with Dylan, our family had slowly but surely begun to heal. With the support of therapists, the guidance of our loved ones, and a renewed determination to move forward, we had weathered the storm and emerged stronger than ever before. The shadows that had once threatened to consume us had been pushed back, replaced by a sense of hope and resilience that filled me with pride.

As I stirred the pizza dough, my mind drifted to the unexpected turn my life had taken. After the tumultuous end of my relationship with Liam, I had found solace in the company of an old friend – Peter, Harley's father. Our interactions had always been cordial, but in the aftermath of the chaos, a deeper connection had blossomed between us.

Peter had been a steady presence, offering a listening ear and a shoulder to lean on when I needed it most. He had been there for Harley, ensuring that my son's needs were met with unwavering care and understanding. And slowly, as we navigated the complexities of co-parenting, I found myself drawn to the man he had become – a devoted father, a loyal friend, and a source of strength in my darkest moments.

It had started with casual conversations, a shared cup of coffee, and the occasional shared meal. But as time passed, the connection between us deepened, and I found myself opening up in ways I hadn't anticipated. Peter was patient, kind, and genuinely interested in my wellbeing, a stark contrast to the turbulence I had experienced with Liam.

One evening, as we sat together on the park bench, watching the children play, Peter had turned to me, his eyes filled with a warmth that made my heart flutter. "Bea," he had said, his voice soft and sincere, "I know things have been difficult, but I want you to know that I'm here for you. Always."

In that moment, the walls I had so carefully constructed began to crumble, and I found myself leaning into his embrace, the weight of the world lifting from my shoulders. It was a tender, unguarded moment, and as our lips met, I felt a sense of peace wash over me, a reminder that even in the darkest of times, there was still the possibility of finding joy and connection.

As I finished preparing the pizza, I couldn't help but smile at the thought of Peter. He had become a constant in my life, a source of stability and comfort that I had desperately needed. With him by my side, I felt stronger, more capable of navigating the challenges that lay ahead.

Just as I was about to call the children for dinner, a sharp knock at the door startled me. I paused, my heart racing, as memories of my father's unexpected visit flooded my mind. Cautiously, I made my way to the front door, peering through the peephole.

To my surprise, it was not my father standing on the doorstep, but rather Liam – the man I had once loved with every fibre of my being. My breath caught in my throat as I took in his familiar features, the anger and anguish etched into his expression. In his hand, I noticed the glint of metal, and my heart sank as I realised he was holding a gun – a sleek, black revolver with a polished finish that sent a chill down my spine.

Steeling my nerves, I opened the door, bracing myself for the confrontation that was sure to follow. "Liam," I said, my voice barely above a whisper. "What are you doing here?"

Liam's eyes narrowed as he stepped forward, his gaze sweeping past me and into the house. "I could ask you the same question," he growled, his voice laced with a mixture of hurt and betrayal. "I just saw you with _him_."

I felt a pang of guilt wash over me, but I refused to back down. "Liam, please, let me explain—"

"Explain what?" he snapped, his voice rising in volume. "How you've moved on? How you've replaced me with _him_?"

I opened my mouth to respond, but before I could, a voice called out from behind me. "Bea? Is everything alright?"

I turned to see Peter standing in the doorway, a concerned expression on his face. Liam's eyes narrowed, and in that moment, I knew that the fragile peace we had built was about to be shattered.

"You," Liam spat, his gaze fixed on Peter. "I should have known you'd be the one to swoop in and take advantage of her."

Peter stepped forward, his posture tensing. "I'm not taking advantage of anyone, Liam. Bea and I—"

"Save it," Liam interrupted, his voice dripping with venom. "I don't want to hear your excuses. You're just another man trying to worm your way into her life, into _my_ family."

The children, drawn by the commotion, began to gather in the hallway, their faces etched with confusion and concern. I felt a surge of panic rise within me, the need to protect them overwhelming.

"Liam, please," I pleaded, stepping between him and Peter. "This isn't the time or place for this. Let's talk about this somewhere else, away from the children."

But Liam was not to be deterred. His eyes blazed with a fury I had never seen before, and in that moment, I knew that the fragile peace we had built was about to be shattered. Suddenly, he raised the gun, the barrel pointed directly at Peter.

"No!" I cried, my voice laced with desperation. "Liam, don't do this!"

The world seemed to slow to a crawl as Liam's finger tightened on the trigger. I lunged forward, desperate to stop him, but I knew I was too late. The deafening crack of the gunshot echoed through the hallway, and I watched in horror as Peter crumpled to the ground, a crimson stain blossoming on his chest.

The children's screams pierced the air, and I felt my heart shatter as I rushed to Peter's side, my hands trembling as I tried to staunch the bleeding. Liam stood frozen, the gun still clutched in his hand, his expression a mix of shock and regret.

In that moment, I knew that our lives had been forever changed. The fragile peace we had built had been shattered, and the future of our family hung in the balance. As I cradled Peter's limp form, the sound of sirens in the distance, I realised that the battle was far from over. The darkness had returned, and this time, I wasn't sure if we had the strength to overcome it.

Chapter 7: Shattered Peace

The deafening crack of the gunshot still echoed in my ears as I cradled Peter's limp form, my hands trembling as I desperately tried to staunch the bleeding. Time seemed to slow to a crawl, the world around me fading into a blur as I focused solely on keeping him alive.

The children's anguished cries pierced the air, their faces etched with pure terror. I spared a glance in their direction, my heart shattering at the sight of their wide, frightened eyes. "Jax, Ariel, Harley - get to your rooms, now!" I yelled, my voice laced with desperation.

Thankfully, they obeyed without hesitation, their small bodies disappearing down the hallway. But as I turned back to Peter, I noticed a familiar face among the chaos – Dylan, his eyes wide with shock and fear.

"Dylan, go with your siblings," I pleaded, my voice cracking. "This isn't something you need to see."

He hesitated for a moment, his gaze fixed on the scene unfolding before him. I could see the wheels turning in his mind, the trauma of his past resurfacing in the wake of this new crisis. But with a deep breath, he nodded and turned, following his siblings to the safety of their rooms.

Turning my attention back to Peter, I pressed harder against the wound, willing the bleeding to stop, but the crimson liquid continued to seep through my fingers. "Hold on, Peter," I pleaded, my voice barely above a whisper. "Help is coming, just hold on."

Liam stood frozen, the gun still clutched in his hand, his expression a mix of shock and regret. I wanted to scream at him, to demand to know what the hell he had done, but in that moment, all that mattered was saving Peter's life.

The sound of sirens in the distance grew louder, and I felt a surge of relief wash over me. "Thank God," I breathed, my eyes never leaving Peter's face. I could see the life slowly draining from him, and I knew that every second counted.

As the police and paramedics finally arrived, the front door burst open, and the hallway erupted into a flurry of activity. Liam was immediately apprehended, the gun wrenched from his grasp as the officers shouted commands.

I barely registered their presence, my focus solely on Peter as the paramedics rushed to his side. They worked quickly, efficiently, their voices calm and authoritative as they barked orders to one another. I held his hand, silently willing him to hold on, to fight for his life.

The minutes ticked by like hours, and I felt the weight of the world pressing down on me. How had everything spiraled so far out of control? We had been on the cusp of a new beginning, and now it all hung in the balance.

As the paramedics prepared to transport Peter to the hospital, I felt a sense of dread wash over me. What if he didn't make it? What would that mean for my family? The uncertainty was overwhelming, and I found myself clinging to the hope that he would pull through.

"Ma'am, we need to get him to the hospital immediately," one of the paramedics said, his voice calm but urgent. "You'll need to ride with us."

I nodded, my legs feeling like lead as I followed them out the door and into the waiting ambulance. As the sirens blared to life, I spared one last glance at the house, at the chaos that had unfolded within its walls.

Liam was being led away, his head bowed, the weight of his actions etched into every line of his body. I felt a pang of sorrow for him, but in that moment, my heart belonged solely to Peter and the uncertain future that lay ahead.

As the ambulance sped through the streets, the world outside a blur of colour and sound, I clutched Peter's hand, silently pleading with the universe to spare his life. This couldn't be how our story ended, not after everything we had been through.

The hospital loomed into view, a beacon of hope in the darkness, and I steeled myself for the battle that was to come. Whatever the outcome, I knew that I would have to be strong, for Peter, for my children, and for the future that hung in the balance.

As the ambulance came to a stop and the doors swung open, I took a deep breath and stepped out into the unknown once again.

Chapter 8: Redemption

The hours that followed were a blur of activity, a whirlwind of doctors, nurses, and endless questions. As Peter was rushed into emergency surgery, I paced the waiting room, my mind racing with a thousand thoughts.

Liam had been taken into custody, the weight of his actions finally catching up to him. I had given a statement to the police, recounting the events that had led to this horrific moment, and I knew that he would face the consequences of his violence.

But in the midst of the chaos, my heart ached for the man I had once loved. Liam had always struggled with his emotions, his temper a constant source of tension in our relationship. I knew that he had never intended to hurt Peter, that the anger and jealousy had simply consumed him in that moment.

As I waited, my thoughts drifted to Dylan, to the way he had frozen in the hallway, his eyes filled with a terror I had hoped he would never have to experience again. I had tried to shield him from the darkness, to protect him from the shadows of my past, and yet here we were, trapped in a new nightmare.

The guilt and anguish threatened to consume me, and I found myself slipping deeper into a well of despair. What if Peter didn't make it? How would I ever be able to face my children, to reassure them that everything would be alright?

Hours turned into days, and as the waiting dragged on, I felt my resolve begin to crumble. The weight of it all became too much to bear, and one night, as I sat alone in the hospital chapel, I made a decision that would change the course of my life forever.

With trembling hands, I reached into my purse and pulled out a small bottle of pills, the contents a deadly cocktail that I had carefully curated. I stared at the bottle, the temptation to end the pain overwhelming, and for a moment, I allowed myself to succumb to the darkness.

But just as I was about to swallow the pills, a voice called out, breaking the silence of the chapel. "Bea?" It was Dylan, his eyes filled with a mixture of concern and understanding.

I froze, the bottle slipping from my grasp as I turned to face my son. In that moment, I saw the pain and anguish reflected in his gaze, a mirror of my own. He knew what I had been about to do, and the realisation of that fact shattered my heart.

"Dylan," I whispered, my voice trembling. "I'm so sorry."

He moved closer, his small hand reaching out to take mine. "Mum, please," he said, his voice barely above a whisper. "Don't do this. We need you."

The weight of his words hit me like a physical blow, and I felt the tears begin to flow. I pulled him into a tight embrace, the bottle of pills forgotten as I clung to him, my sobs echoing through the empty chapel.

In that moment, I knew that I had to be strong, not just for Dylan, but for all of my children. They needed me, and I couldn't give in to the darkness, not when they were counting on me to guide them through this storm.

With a renewed sense of purpose, I made my way back to the hospital, determined to be there for Peter, to support him in his recovery. The road ahead would not be an easy one, but I knew that with the love and strength of my family, we could overcome even the greatest of challenges.

As I entered Peter's room, I was greeted by the sight of him, battered and bruised, but alive. The relief that washed over me was palpable, and I rushed to his bedside, taking his hand in mine.

"Peter," I whispered, my voice thick with emotion. "I'm here. I'm not going anywhere."

He opened his eyes, a weak smile tugging at the corners of his lips. "Bea," he breathed, his voice barely audible. "I'm so glad you're safe."

I felt a surge of gratitude and love wash over me, and in that moment, I knew that I had found the strength to fight for our future. Liam may have been the one who pulled the trigger, but it was Peter who had truly saved me, his unwavering support and love a beacon in the darkness.

As I sat by his bedside, holding his hand and whispering words of encouragement, I knew that the road ahead would be long and difficult. But with Peter by my side, and the love and support of my family, I was ready to face it head-on.

The road to redemption would not be an easy one, but I was determined to see it through, to reclaim the life that had been stolen from us. Liam would face the consequences of his actions, and I would ensure that my children were protected, that they never had to experience the darkness that had once consumed our lives.

The years that followed were a whirlwind of emotions, a constant dance between the darkness and the light. As Peter recovered from his injuries, our family slowly began to heal, each of us finding our own way to navigate the aftermath of the devastating events that had unfolded.

Jax, our eldest, had grown into a vibrant young man, his laughter and boundless energy a welcome respite from the lingering shadows. I would watch him for hours, marveling at the resilience he had shown, the way he seemed to bounce back from the trauma with a resilience that left me in awe.

The twins, Olly and Harry, had blossomed as well, their once-withdrawn demeanours replaced by confident, outgoing young individuals. Gone were the days of constant worry, the fear that they might not make it through the night. The baby monitors had long since been packed away, a testament to the resilience and strength of our little ones.

Harley focused on his studies, putting all his energy into schoolwork. This helped him stay grounded. Meanwhile, Ariel, our sweet and sensitive daughter, struggled with her past scars. Though she had found solace in the arts, her creativity a shining light in the darkness, the trauma of that fateful night still lingered, manifesting in moments of anxiety and fear. I watched her with a heavy heart, my own guilt and anguish weighing heavily on me, as I tried to guide her through the challenges she faced.

And then there was Dylan – my sweet, troubled son, who had once been consumed by the darkness. He had come a long way, his progress marked by small but significant steps. He had started attending school full-time, immersing himself in a routine that provided structure and stability.

I had wanted to share our story, to use my experiences to educate others about the devastating impact of abuse. But as time passed, I found myself pulling back, the weight of it all becoming too much to bear. Instead, I focused on my family, on rebuilding the life that had been shattered.

As time passed however, I found myself pulled in a new direction, one that threatened to unravel the fragile peace we had built. It started innocently enough, a way to pass the time and distract myself from the lingering pain. But as the wins started to pile up, I found myself drawn deeper and deeper into the allure of easy money.

I kept it hidden from Peter, convinced that I could control it, that I could walk away at any time. But the truth was, the gambling had become a crutch, a way to numb the guilt and the fear that still haunted me. And as the stakes grew higher, I found myself spiralling, the weight of my secret threatening to consume me.

The thrill of the win, the rush of adrenaline, became an addiction that I couldn't shake. I would spend hours at the casino, my mind consumed by the flashing lights and the sound of the slots. It was a way to escape the reality of my life, to forget the pain and the trauma that had shaped me.

But as the losses mounted, the guilt and shame became overwhelming. I found myself dipping into our savings, desperate to recoup my losses and keep the secret hidden. The lies grew more elaborate, the excuses more elaborate, and I could feel the trust between Peter and I beginning to fray.

I knew that I was spiralling out of control, that the gambling was threatening to destroy everything I had fought so hard to build. But the allure of the casino, the promise of a quick fix, was too strong to resist. I became consumed by the need to win, to prove to myself that I could be in control, that I could overcome the darkness that had haunted me for so long.

The nights spent at the betting shops, the hours spent glued to the screen, became a blur of desperation and regret. I would come home, exhausted and defeated, only to face the worried eyes of my children. I wanted to stop, to walk away, but the hold of the addiction was too strong.

It wasn't until I hit rock bottom, until I found myself standing in the hospital chapel, a bottle of pills in my hand, that I finally realised the true cost of my actions. The guilt and the shame had become too much to bear, and in that moment, I knew that I had to find the strength to break free.

With Peter's support, I began the long and arduous journey of recovery. It was a battle, a constant struggle against the demons that threatened to pull me back into the depths of despair. But with each step forward, I felt a glimmer of hope, a reminder that I was not alone, that there was a way out of the darkness.

I eventually found the strength to break free. And as I watched my children grow and thrive, I knew that the sacrifices I had made were worth it, that the battle had been worth fighting.

The road to redemption was long and winding, but with each step forward, I felt a sense of peace and clarity that I had never known before. The darkness may have threatened to consume me, but in the end, it was the light of my family that guided me through the storm.

It was during this time that I faced Liam in court, the confrontation a brutal reminder of the trauma we had all endured. I had steeled myself, determined to stand tall and face him, to show him that he no longer had power over us.

But as I stood there, his eyes boring into mine, I felt the walls I had so carefully constructed begin to crumble. The memories of our past, the love and the pain, all came rushing back, and in that moment, I knew that I would never be free of the bond we shared.

"Liam," I had said, my voice trembling, "I will never forgive you for what you've done. But I want you to know that a part of me will always care for you, especially when it comes to Scarlett."

He had stared at me, his expression unreadable, and in that moment, I saw a glimmer of the man I had once loved. It was a fleeting moment, but it was enough to remind me that even in the darkest of times, there was still the possibility of redemption.

As the verdict was read and Liam was sentenced, I felt a weight lift from my shoulders. It was over, the chapter finally closed, and as I left the courtroom, I knew that I had to find a way to move forward, for the sake of my family.

It was then that I turned to Peter, my rock, my constant. He had been there for me through it all, his unwavering support and love a beacon in the darkness. And despite the secrets I had kept, the lies I had told, he still welcomed me with open arms.

Together, we worked to rebuild our lives, to create a future that was filled with hope and possibility. Peter understood the pull of the gambling, the way it had become a crutch for me, and he supported me every step of the way as I fought to break free of its grip.

It was a long and arduous process, but with Peter by my side, I found the strength to confront my demons, to face the darkness head-on. And as I did, I watched as my children blossomed, each one finding their own way to heal and grow.

Jax, now a vibrant young man, filled our home with laughter and joy, his bond with his siblings growing stronger with each passing day. Olly, Harry, and Harley thrived, showing talents that made us proud. My sweet, resilient son Dylan also found his way. His focus and determination proved the strength of family and love.

And though Ariel still struggled with the scars of her past, her resilience and determination to overcome her challenges filled me with a sense of pride and hope. I knew that the road ahead would not be an easy one, but with the love and support of our family, I was confident that she would find the strength to heal and thrive.

As the years passed, I watched my children grow and thrive, their resilience and strength a testament to the power of love and family. And though the scars of the past would never fully heal, I knew that we had emerged stronger, more resilient than ever before.

Peter, too, had made a full recovery, his injuries a distant memory as he embraced the role of devoted father and partner. He forgave Liam. He understood the deep pain that led to Liam's desperate act. Their relationship, though strained, changed into one of mutual respect and understanding.

And as for me, I had finally found the courage to confront my own demons, to break free of the hold that the gambling had on me. It had been a long and difficult journey, but with the unwavering support of my family, I had emerged victorious, my future once again filled with hope and possibility.

Epilogue: As I sat on the porch, watching my children play in the warm summer breeze, I couldn't help but feel a profound sense of gratitude. We had weathered the storm, and though the path ahead was still uncertain, I knew that we would face it together, our bond stronger than ever before.

In that moment, I glanced over to where Peter sat, a warm smile playing on his lips as he observed the children's laughter and joy. The journey to this point had not been an easy one for him, the physical and emotional scars of that fateful day still evident. I remembered how arduous his recovery had been, the long months of physiotherapy and the constant pain that lingered in his movements. There were times when I feared he might not regain the full mobility and strength he had once possessed, but his resilience and determination had been an inspiration to us all.

Now, as I watched him interact with the children, I marvelled at how far he had come. The limp that had once slowed his gait had become barely perceptible, a subtle reminder of the trauma he had endured. And while the gunshot wound had left a jagged scar across his chest, it no longer seemed to trouble him as he moved with an effortless grace.

Just a few months ago, Peter had made the decision to leave his previous job, feeling that the demands and stresses were no longer a good fit for him in the aftermath of his injury. It had been a bold move, one that had caused some initial concern, but I had witnessed the transformation in him as he explored new avenues.

Now, he had found a position at a local community centre, where he worked tirelessly to support those in need. His empathy and understanding, forged through his own struggles, had become a wellspring of strength for others. I watched as he engaged with the teenagers in the centre, guiding them with a gentle hand and a compassionate ear, and I felt a swell of pride in my chest.

As he caught my gaze, his eyes shone with a contentment I had not seen in a long time. The weight of the past had not been erased, but it no longer seemed to burden him as it once had. Instead, there was a newfound lightness to his spirit, a resilience that had been tempered by the fires of adversity.

In that moment, I knew that the darkness had been vanquished, replaced by a renewed appreciation for the beauty and wonder of life. The future seemed uncertain, but we were ready. We wanted to write a new chapter in our lives. This chapter would celebrate resilience, the beauty of forgiveness, and our strong family bond.

Printed in Great Britain
by Amazon